A YOUNG WITCH'S GUIDE

To the Moon Stars & Lunar Magic

WILHELMINA WOODS

To the dreamers, the stargazers,

and the moonlight seekers

This book is for you.

May you always find magic in the stars,

wonder in the moon's glow,

and the courage to embrace the witch within you.

Shine brightly, little Moon witch.

The universe is yours to explore.

Book Cover by Tukotuku Publishing

Illustrations by Tukotuku Publishing

First edition 2024

Print   978-1-991306-89-0
Ebook   978-1-991306-90-6

CONTENTS

A Magical Journey

Beneath the Moon and Stars

Welcome, young Witch! If you've ever looked up at the night sky and felt a mysterious pull toward the Moon and stars, you're already in touch with the magic that surrounds us. There's something enchanting about the way the Moon glows, lighting up the darkness and painting the sky with a silver sheen. It whispers secrets to those who listen, guiding new Witches like you on their magical path.

In this book, you'll discover how to harness the moon's power, connect with the stars, and embrace the beautiful, magical energy they provide. Whether you're just starting your journey or have already begun to dabble in witch-craft, this guide will introduce you to the mystical realm of lunar magic, teach you how to work with Moon phases, and show you how the stars can be your celestial companions. So, take a deep breath, open your heart to the magic of the universe, and let's begin our journey into the wonders of the Moon and stars.

The Moon: Your First Magical Ally

In the magical world, the Moon is one of our greatest allies. She has a calming, nurturing presence, guiding us through darkness and illuminating our path when we feel lost. The moon's phases – from the slender crescent to the glowing full Moon and back again – mirror the cycles of life. By aligning our magic with the moon's energy, we can create spells, rituals, and practices that flow with the natural rhythms of the universe.

But why the moon, you may ask? Throughout history, Witches and wise ones have looked to the Moon for guidance. Her ever-changing face reminds us of the constant ebb and flow of life. Just as the Moon waxes and wanes, grows full, and disappears, so do our own feelings, thoughts, and energies. When you learn to understand the moon's phases, you'll begin to recognize how they influence not just the tides and nature around us but also your inner world. You'll become more attuned to when to start new ventures, when to focus on self-care, and when to let go of things that no longer serve you.

In this guide, we will explore each phase of the Moon and how it can be used in your witchcraft practice. You'll learn about rituals to perform under the new moon, spells to cast during the full moon, and even how to use the moon's energy to help manifest your dreams. By the end of this book, you'll feel a deep connection with the Moon and her magical rhythms.

Star Magic: Wishing Upon the Night Sky

While the Moon lights up our nights, the stars sprinkle magic across the sky. Have you ever wished upon a shooting star or gazed up at constellations, feeling a sense of wonder and mystery? Stars have been used for centuries by sailors for navigation, by astrologers to read destinies, and by Witches to connect with the universe. In this book, we'll explore the magic of stars, how they can guide us, and how to incorporate their energy into our spells.

Each star holds its own unique energy, and by learning to connect with the stars, you can invite their wisdom and guidance into your life. You'll discover how to identify key constellations, how to create star charms for protection, and even how to draw on the energy of the stars for powerful magical workings. The night sky is full of wonder, and every time you look up, you're gazing into a world brimming with ancient magic.

Lunar Cycles: Riding the Waves of Moon Phases

One of the most magical aspects of working with the Moon is understanding her cycles. The Moon goes through phases, just like you do, and each phase carries its own special energy. The new Moon is a time for fresh starts, new intentions, and planting the seeds of your dreams. As the Moon waxes, or grows, its energy builds, helping you work on manifesting those dreams. The full Moon is the peak of this energy, a time of celebration, power, and magic. After the full moon, the waning phase begins, where it's time to release and let go of anything holding you back.

This cycle repeats every month, offering you a natural rhythm to work with in your magical practice. In this book, we'll dive deep into each phase, giving you the tools to create Moon phase rituals, use the moon's energy for spells, and harness its power to support your magical journey. The moon's phases are like the tides – they ebb and flow, teaching us when to draw things into our lives and when to let go. By tuning into these cycles, you'll be able to create magic that feels effortless and aligned with the universe's rhythms.

Magic Tools: Moon Water, Crystals, and Star Charms

Every Witch needs their magical tools, and this guidebook will introduce you to some of the most enchanting ones connected with the Moon and stars. You'll learn how to make Moon water – a powerful magical tool created by leaving water under the moonlight to absorb its energy. We'll explore lunar crystals, like moonstone and selenite, and how to charge them under the Moon to amplify their powers.

But that's not all. The stars offer their own kind of magic, and you'll discover how to create star charms, use celestial symbols, and even call upon star spirits to guide and protect you. These tools are simple yet powerful, perfect for a young Witch starting her journey. As you work with these magical items, you'll feel more connected to the Moon and stars, enhancing your spells and rituals.

Your Magical Journey Begins Now

As you journey through this book, you'll find that Moon and star magic is about more than just spells and rituals – it's about forming a relationship with the universe. It's about standing beneath the night sky, feeling the moon's light on your skin, and knowing that you are a part of something ancient, beautiful, and endlessly magical. You'll learn how to use lunar magic to support your dreams, nurture your emotions, and guide you through life's ups and downs.

This guidebook is designed to be your companion as you step into the world of lunar and celestial witchcraft. Whether you're creating your first Moon water, performing a full Moon ritual, or simply stargazing and feeling the magic of the night, you're tapping into a powerful force that has been used by Witches for centuries. And now, it's your turn to embrace this magic and make it your own.

So, grab your journal, find a cozy spot under the night sky, and get ready to explore the magical realm of the Moon and stars. Your journey as a Moon Witch begins now, and with each chapter, you'll feel the Moon and stars guiding you, filling your heart with magic, and lighting your path. Let's explore the wonders of lunar magic together!

THE MAGIC OF THE MOON

T he Moon has always been a symbol of magic, mystery, and change. When you look up at the sky at night and see that glowing orb, you're not just seeing a chunk of rock floating in space. You're seeing one of the most powerful forces of nature, one that has inspired witches, dreamers, and seekers of magic for thousands of years. Understanding the moon's energy is the first step on your magical journey as a young witch. Let's explore why the Moon is so magical, how its phases affect our world, and how you can connect with its energy to enhance your spells and rituals.

Have you ever noticed how the Moon changes shape from night to night? Sometimes it's a thin crescent, sometimes it's half-full, and other times, it's a bright, glowing ball lighting up the sky. These changes aren't just beautiful to look at; they also have a deep, magical significance. The

Moon goes through a cycle, called the lunar cycle, which lasts about 29 days. During this time, the Moon moves through different phases, and each phase carries its own unique energy.

The Moon has a powerful influence on Earth. It affects the tides, pulling the oceans up and down, which is why we have high and low tides. But it's not just the oceans that feel the moon's pull. The Moon also affects plants, animals, and even us! Think about it: your body is made up of about 60% water. Just like the ocean, the water in your body responds to the moon's energy, which is why many people feel different emotions, thoughts, and even physical changes depending on the moon's phase. This is one of the reasons why the Moon is so magical in witchcraft—it's a powerful, ever-present force that affects the world around us and within us.

In witchcraft, the Moon is often seen as a symbol of intuition, emotion, and the subconscious mind. You know those gut feelings you sometimes get, or the dreams that feel so real you almost think they're trying to tell you something? That's the moon's influence, guiding you to listen to your inner voice. Witches have been working with the moon's energy for centuries, using its phases to time their spells, rituals, and intentions. When you work with the moon, you're not just practicing magic; you're aligning with the natural rhythms of the universe.

Let's dive into the moon's phases and how they each have their own magical energy. The moon's cycle begins with the **new Moon,** which is when the Moon is barely visible in the sky. The new Moon is all about new beginnings, fresh starts, and setting intentions. This is a great time to think about what you want to invite into your life. Maybe you want to start a new project, develop a new habit, or set a goal. During the new moon, take a moment to sit quietly, close your eyes, and picture what you want to achieve. This is called setting an intention. Writing your intentions down in a special journal or on a piece of paper makes them even more powerful. It's like planting a seed in your mind, giving it the chance to grow.

After the new Moon comes the **waxing crescent Moon,** where you'll see a small sliver of light in the sky. This phase is perfect for building energy and nurturing the intentions you set during the new moon. Think of this phase as watering the seed you planted. Use this time to take small steps toward your goals. If you set an intention for more self-care, now is the time to start adding small acts of kindness to yourself into your daily routine. As the Moon grows, or "waxes," its energy strengthens, helping you focus and build momentum.

Next, we have the **first quarter Moon,** which looks like half of a Moon shining in the sky. This is a time of action and decision-making. The first quarter Moon is all about facing challenges and moving forward. Sometimes, when you're working toward a goal, obstacles pop up. Maybe you're feeling unsure or facing difficulties. The first quarter moon's energy gives you the strength to push through. This is a great time to do spells or rituals for courage, confidence, and determination. Remind yourself that you're capable of overcoming challenges and keep going!

The Moon then moves into the **waxing gibbous phase**, where it's nearly full. This phase is all about refining and perfecting. The Moon is building up to its full power, and so are you! Use this time to review your progress, make adjustments, and put the finishing touches on whatever you've been working toward. If you've been practicing spells, now is the time to charge your tools and gather your magical supplies for the upcoming full moon. The waxing gibbous Moon encourages you to stay focused and patient because something magical is about to happen.

Then, we reach the **full Moon**—the most powerful and magical phase of the lunar cycle. The full Moon is bright, glowing, and full of energy. It's a time of celebration, manifestation, and abundance. When the Moon is full, it's at the peak of its power, which means it can amplify whatever energy you're working with. This is a fantastic time to perform spells for manifesting your desires, charging your crystals, or simply expressing gratitude for the blessings in your life. The full moon's light also helps you see things more clearly, making it a great time for self-reflection and gaining insight into your inner thoughts and feelings.

After the full moon, the Moon starts to shrink, or "wane." The **waning gibbous Moon** comes next, and it's all about releasing and letting go. Just like a flower eventually sheds its petals, this phase is about letting go of what no longer serves you. Maybe there are habits, thoughts, or emotions that are holding you back. The waning gibbous moon's energy supports spells and rituals for releasing negativity, breaking bad habits, or clearing your space of stagnant energy.

Following this phase is the **last quarter Moon**, which looks like half of a Moon in the sky, but this time it's shrinking. The last quarter Moon is a time for forgiveness, clearing out, and finishing up loose ends. It's a great time to cleanse your space, tie up any unfinished business, and forgive yourself or others for mistakes made. This phase encourages you to make peace with things that didn't go as planned and prepare for a fresh start.

Finally, we come to the **waning crescent Moon**, where only a small sliver of light is left. This phase is all about rest, reflection, and renewal. Just as plants go dormant in the winter before blooming in the spring, you need time to rest and recharge before starting a new cycle. Use this phase to relax, meditate, and think about what you've learned. Take care of yourself, nurture your body and mind, and get ready for the new Moon to begin the cycle once more.

Now that you understand the moon's phases and their energies, how do you connect with these lunar vibes in your witchcraft practice? One of the simplest ways to start is to go outside and spend time Moon gazing. Find a quiet spot where you can look up at the Moon and soak in its light. As you gaze at the moon, pay attention to how you feel. Are you feeling calm? Energized? Reflective? The moon's energy will speak to you in its own way, helping you tune into your intuition.

Another wonderful way to connect with lunar energy is to keep a Moon journal. In your journal, you can record your feelings, dreams, and magical experiences during each Moon phase. Over time, you'll start to notice patterns and learn how the moon's energy affects you. You can also use your journal to write down intentions during the new Moon and reflect on your progress as the cycle continues.

THE MOON HAS SO MUCH WISDOM AND MAGIC TO SHARE. BY UNDERSTANDING ITS PHASES AND ALIGNING WITH ITS ENERGY, YOU'RE STEPPING INTO A WORLD WHERE NATURE AND MAGIC WORK HAND IN HAND. THE MOON IS HERE TO GUIDE YOU, TO LIGHT YOUR PATH, AND TO HELP YOU HARNESS YOUR INNER POWER. SO, THE NEXT TIME YOU LOOK UP AT THE MOON, REMEMBER: YOU'RE NOT JUST A WITCH—YOU'RE A MOON WITCH, AND THE MAGIC OF THE UNIVERSE IS AT YOUR FINGERTIPS.

The Moon in
Witchcraft

The Moon has always been a source of magic, mystery, and power in the world of witchcraft. For centuries, Witches and wise ones have looked to the Moon for guidance, healing, and strength. The moon's gentle glow at night isn't just a beautiful sight; it holds a deep connection to the Earth and everything living on it. As a young witch, learning about the history of Moon magic, the goddesses associated with the moon, and how different cultures honor it will help you understand the depth of this ancient power and how you can harness it in your own practice.

The history of Moon magic is almost as old as time itself. In ancient times, people quickly noticed how the Moon affected the world around them. They saw how the moon's phases controlled the ocean tides, influenced plant growth, and even seemed to change people's moods. This led them to believe that the Moon must be magical, a force to be respected and honored. Early Witches and wise ones began to study the moon's phases and developed rituals and spells that aligned with its energy. They learned that certain phases of the Moon were better for planting crops, setting intentions, and even performing certain types of magic.

In ancient Mesopotamia, one of the earliest known civilizations, people worshipped the Moon as a powerful goddess. They believed that the Moon had the power to watch over the night, protect travelers, and control the rhythm of life. In ancient Egypt, the Moon was associated with the goddess Isis, who was known for her magical abilities and protective nature. Witches would call upon the energy of the Moon to help them with their spells, rituals, and healing practices. They believed that working with the moon's cycles could help them align with the natural flow of the universe, making their magic stronger and more effective.

The Greeks and Romans also had a deep respect for the moon, linking it to goddesses like Selene, Artemis, and Diana. They believed that these Moon goddesses had the power to watch over the world, protect animals, and guide those who traveled at night. In Greek mythology, Selene was known as the personification of the moon, a beautiful goddess who rode her chariot across the night sky. Artemis, another Greek goddess, was associated with the Moon and was known as the protector of wild animals, forests, and young women. Witches would invoke

Artemis's energy when they needed courage, strength, or protection.

But Moon magic isn't just a part of Western history. It's a universal practice found in cultures all around the world. In China, for example, the Moon is honored during the Mid-Autumn Festival, a celebration of the harvest and family unity. During this festival, people light lanterns, share mooncakes, and gaze at the full moon, thanking it for its blessings. The Chinese goddess Chang'e is often associated with the moon. According to legend, she lives on the Moon and is a symbol of beauty, grace, and the mysterious nature of the night.

In Japan, the Moon is admired during a celebration known as Tsukimi, or "Moon viewing." This tradition dates back over a thousand years, and people gather to watch the full moon, decorate their homes with pampas grass, and make offerings of rice dumplings called dango. Japanese culture sees the Moon as a symbol of beauty, transformation, and the passage of time, reflecting its influence in poetry, art, and spirituality.

The Māori people of New Zealand also have their own Moon magic traditions. They honor the Moon goddess, Hina, a powerful figure in Māori mythology. Hina is often considered the goddess of the Moon and the tides, controlling the cycles of nature and guiding the growth of plants. Māori people use the lunar calendar, called Maramataka, to plan their activities, such as planting crops, fishing, and gathering food. They believe that each phase of the Moon has a different energy that affects the land and sea. For example, the new moon, or Whiro, is seen as a time for planning and quiet reflection, while the full moon, known as Rakaunui, is a time of celebration, abundance, and the best time for harvesting.

Learning about Moon goddesses is another important part of Moon magic. Many cultures have associated the Moon with powerful female deities who embody the moon's energy, wisdom, and beauty. In ancient times, these goddesses were called upon for protection, guidance, and help in navigating the mysteries of life. Knowing about these goddesses can help you connect with the moon's magic on a deeper level, as they represent different aspects of the moon's power.

One of the most well-known Moon goddesses is Selene from Greek mythology. Selene was seen as the personification of the moon, riding her chariot across the sky each night. She was known for her glowing beauty and her deep connection to the cycles of life. Witches would call upon Selene's energy for guidance, intuition, and to harness the moon's magical power. Her presence reminds us of the importance of embracing our emotions, dreams, and inner wisdom.

Another Moon goddess you might find inspiring is Artemis, the Greek goddess of the hunt, wilderness, and the moon. Artemis is known for her fierce independence, bravery, and protective nature. She was a guardian of animals, forests, and young girls, embodying the strength and wild beauty of the natural world. When you call upon Artemis in your Moon rituals, you're connecting with her energy of courage, confidence, and the power of nature. She teaches us that the Moon is not just gentle and soft but also strong and bold, reminding us to embrace all aspects of our magical selves.

In Roman mythology, the Moon goddess Diana was similar to Artemis. She was the goddess of the moon, the hunt, and wild animals. Diana was often worshipped in forests and at crossroads, places where the veil between the physical and spiritual worlds is thin. Many Witches today honor Diana as a protector and guide, especially during full Moon rituals, as her energy is believed to be strongest when the Moon is at its peak.

And then there's Hina, the Māori Moon goddess, who represents the nurturing, cyclical power of the moon. In some stories, Hina is said to have traveled to the Moon to escape difficulties on Earth, finding peace and solitude in the moon's embrace. She symbolizes the moon's quiet strength, the ability to adapt and change while maintaining a steady presence. When you connect with Hina, you're embracing the moon's role as a constant guide in the ever-changing world, reminding you to find balance and harmony within yourself.

The Moon also plays a central role in many different cultures' magical and spiritual practices. In Hindu tradition, the moon, or Chandra, is associated with emotions, the mind, and fertility. The Moon is considered a god who controls the tides and is linked to the life cycles of plants, animals, and humans. Hindu Witches and spiritual practitioners perform rituals based on the lunar calendar, celebrating special days like Purnima (full moon) to honor its influence. During these times, offerings are made to the Moon to seek blessings, healing, and wisdom.

In Native American traditions, many tribes have their own unique Moon rituals and beliefs. Some tribes, like the Ojibwe and Cree, use the lunar calendar to mark the passing of time, naming each full Moon according to the natural events that occur during that month. For example, the Wolf Moon in January signals the time when wolves are most active, while the Harvest Moon in September marks the peak of the harvest season. These names reflect the deep connection between the moon, the Earth, and the cycles of nature.

In Wicca, a modern form of witchcraft, the Moon is honored in rituals known as Esbats. Esbats are held during the full Moon and sometimes on other Moon phases to celebrate the moon's energy and use its power for magical workings. Wiccans believe that the Moon represents the goddess, the divine feminine, and its phases symbolize the cycle of life: birth, growth, death, and rebirth. By aligning their magic with the moon's phases, Wiccans strengthen their spells and deepen their connection to the natural world.

All of these different cultures, myths, and traditions show how deeply the Moon is woven into the fabric of our world and the magical practices of Witches throughout history. When you honor the moon, you're connecting with an ancient power that crosses time, space, and cultures. By understanding the moon's history, the goddesses associated with it, and the ways it has been celebrated around the world, you open yourself up to its wisdom and strength.

As you continue your journey as a young witch, remember that the Moon is always there for you, a constant companion lighting up the night. Whether you call upon the energy of Selene, Artemis, Hina, or simply the Moon itself, you're tapping into a well of magic that has been cherished and used by Witches for centuries. The Moon invites you to explore its mysteries, embrace its cycles, and find your own rhythm within its glowing light. The more you learn about the moon's magic, the more you'll discover how it can guide you, protect you, and help you navigate the magical path that lies ahead.

THE MOON AND YOUR MAGIC

The Moon is a powerful ally in witchcraft, and understanding how to work with its phases can make your spells more effective and meaningful. As you grow in your practice, you'll find that aligning your magic with the moon's cycles can amplify the energy of your intentions and help you connect more deeply with the natural world. In this chapter, we're going to explore how to use the moon's phases in your spells, the importance of setting intentions with the new moon, and the power of releasing energy during the full moon.

Witches have been using the phases of the Moon for centuries, as each phase holds a unique energy that you can tap into for different types of spells and rituals. The Moon goes through its full cycle every 29 days, moving from new Moon to full Moon and back again. By understanding the magic of each phase, you can choose the perfect time for your spells, whether you're looking to attract something new into your life or let go of things that no longer serve you.

When the Moon is new, it's a time of beginnings and fresh starts. This is when the sky is darkest, and the Moon is just a sliver of light, signaling the start of a new cycle. Because of this, the new Moon is an excellent time for setting intentions and starting new projects. Think of the new Moon as a blank canvas or a seed waiting to be planted. During this phase, you can focus on what you want to grow or manifest in your life. Setting intentions is a way to tell the universe what you want to work toward, and doing so during the new Moon gives your intentions that extra magical boost.

The waxing moon, which follows the new moon, is when the Moon grows bigger in the sky. This phase is all about building energy and taking action. It's a time for spells that focus on growth, strength, and attracting positive things into your life. If you've set an intention during the new moon, the waxing phase is when you start putting effort into making that intention come to life. For example, if your intention was to bring more confidence into your life, the waxing Moon is the perfect time to practice self-love rituals, speak positive affirmations, or wear crystals that boost confidence.

When the Moon reaches its full phase, it shines bright and powerful, filling the sky with its glow. The full Moon is a time of celebration, manifestation, and heightened energy. This is when the moon's power is at its peak, and any magic you perform under the full Moon is super-charged. The full Moon is perfect for spells that focus on bringing your dreams to fruition, charging magical tools like crystals, and releasing any negative energy that's been building up.

After the full moon, the Moon begins to wane, or shrink. This waning phase is about letting go and releasing. It's the perfect time for banishing spells, releasing bad habits, and clearing away anything that might be holding you back. As the Moon gets smaller, it takes away the energy of what you want to release, helping you create space for new beginnings. Working with the moon's phases like this helps you connect with nature's cycles and makes your magic more in tune with the world around you.

One of the most powerful ways to work with the Moon is by setting intentions during the new moon. The new Moon is all about starting fresh, so it's the perfect time to think about what you want to bring into your life. Setting an intention is like planting a seed in the universe. When you focus your thoughts and energy on something you want, you're telling the universe that you're ready for it. This is a key part of manifesting your desires.

To set your intention during the new moon, find a quiet place where you won't be disturbed. You can do this inside or outside, under the night sky if possible. Close your eyes, take a few deep breaths, and think about what you truly want to attract into your life. It might be a new friendship, more self-confidence, better grades in school, or a new hobby you want to explore. Whatever it is, picture it clearly in your mind. Imagine how it would feel to have this wish come true. Let that feeling fill you up.

When you have a clear idea of your intention, write it down on a piece of paper or in a special journal. Writing your intention helps you focus your thoughts and sends a message to the universe that you're serious about what you want. As you write, be specific and positive. For example, instead of writing "I don't want to be shy," try "I am growing more confident every day." Words carry energy, so make sure to use ones that reflect what you want to create.

After you've written your intention, say it out loud. Speaking your intention gives it life and power. You might say something like, "Under this new moon, I set my intention to grow more confident and believe in myself." You can then fold your paper and place it somewhere special, like under your pillow, in a box, or on your altar if you have one. Each day, as the Moon grows, take small actions that support your intention. This could be practicing positive self-talk, trying something new, or stepping out of your comfort zone. As the Moon waxes, your intention gains energy, moving closer to becoming a reality.

The full Moon is just as important as the new Moon when it comes to your magical practice. This phase is the peak of the moon's power, making it an ideal time to release what no longer serves you and amplify the things you want to manifest. During the full moon, the energy is vibrant and strong, so it's the perfect time to do spells for charging, cleansing, and letting go.

One of the most popular full Moon practices is releasing energy that might be holding you back. Over time, we all collect energy from our surroundings, and not all of it is positive. Thoughts, worries, negative habits, or even clutter in our space can create blocks that keep us from reaching our goals. The full Moon is like a cosmic eraser, helping us clear away those blocks and make room for new, positive energy.

To release energy during the full moon, start by making a list of things you want to let go of. This might include negative thoughts, fears, worries, or habits you've outgrown. Write them down honestly. There's no right or wrong answer here—it's all about what feels heavy or unhelpful to you. Once you have your list, take it outside under the light of the full moon. Find a quiet spot where you can be alone with your thoughts.

Close your eyes and take a few deep breaths, feeling the moon's light on your skin. Imagine the moon's energy washing over you, clearing away all the things you want to release. You might even picture the Moon pulling away those worries, like waves taking away sand on the beach. When you feel ready, read your list out loud. As you speak, imagine each item dissolving into the moonlight, leaving you lighter and freer.

After you've spoken your intentions, you can safely burn the paper (if it's safe to do so) or tear it into tiny pieces.

This act symbolizes letting go and releasing the old energy. As you watch the paper burn or the pieces scatter, thank the Moon for its help in clearing your path. You might say, "I release what no longer serves me under this full moon. I am free to embrace new beginnings." This ritual allows you to start fresh with a clear mind and open heart.

You can also use the full moon's energy to charge your magical tools. Crystals, tarot cards, and other objects you use in your practice can absorb energy from their surroundings over time, so it's a good idea to cleanse them regularly. The full moon's light is perfect for this. Simply place your items outside or on a windowsill where the moonlight can touch them. Leave them there overnight to soak up the moon's powerful energy. The next morning, you'll find your tools feeling refreshed, recharged, and ready for magic.

Working with the Moon in your magical practice helps you connect with the natural cycles of the world and your own inner power. By using the phases of the moon, setting intentions during the new moon, and releasing energy during the full moon, you're tuning into a rhythm that has guided Witches for generations. The Moon is a wise teacher, reminding us that life is full of cycles—of growth, release, and renewal. As you follow the moon's path, you'll find that your magic becomes stronger, more focused, and more aligned with your heart's desires. The Moon is your guide, lighting up the night and helping you navigate the world of witchcraft with confidence and grace.

PHASES OF THE MOON AND THEIR POWERS

O ne of the most magical aspects of being a Witch is working with the different phases of the moon. Each phase has its own special energy that you can harness to enhance your spells and rituals. In this chapter, we're going to explore the waxing moon—a time of growth, action, and attraction. The waxing Moon is like a magical friend who helps you build momentum toward your dreams. Let's dive into what the waxing Moon is, how you can connect with its energy, and which spells are best suited for this powerful phase.

The waxing Moon begins just after the new Moon and lasts until the full moon. During this time, the Moon gradually grows in size, shining more brightly each night. If you look up at the sky during the waxing moon, you'll notice that it's getting bigger and brighter as it makes its way toward becoming a full moon. This is why it's called the "waxing" moon; it's the time when the Moon is increasing or "growing." The energy of the waxing Moon is all about building, growing, and moving forward. It's like planting a seed and watching it sprout into a strong, healthy plant. When you work with the waxing moon's energy, you're tapping into that natural momentum to bring your intentions and dreams to life.

The waxing Moon is a perfect time for setting goals and taking action steps toward what you want to achieve. Think of it as the phase where you "water your seeds" and nurture your intentions so they can grow strong. If you set an intention during the new moon, the waxing Moon is when you start putting that intention into motion. For example, if your new Moon intention was to build more self-confidence, the waxing Moon is the time to practice self-love, positive affirmations, and small steps that make you feel more confident each day.

During the waxing moon, the energy in the universe is building up, just like the moon's light. This means it's an ideal time for spells and rituals that focus on growth, attraction, and taking action. If there's something you want to attract into your life, such as love, friendship, creativity, or success, the waxing Moon will give your magic an extra boost. This is the time to be bold, take action, and put your intentions out into the world.

One way to connect with the waxing Moon is through rituals that celebrate growth and progress. These rituals don't have to be complicated; they can be simple yet powerful ways to align with the waxing moon's energy. A wonderful ritual to try during the waxing Moon is a "growth jar." This ritual is designed to help you focus on what you want to grow in your life, whether it's confidence, friendships, skills, or even your own magical practice.

To create a growth jar, you'll need a small glass jar, a piece of paper, a pen, and some dried herbs or flowers (like rosemary, lavender, or rose petals). Sit in a quiet place where you won't be disturbed. Take a few deep breaths, and think about what you want to grow in your life. It could be anything that makes you feel happy, empowered, or connected. Once you have your intention in mind, write it down on the piece of paper. Be as clear and specific as possible. For example, you might write, "I am growing in confidence and love for myself each day."

After you've written your intention, fold the paper and place it inside the jar. Add the dried herbs or flowers, filling the jar with the energy of growth and beauty. As you do this, imagine your intention growing stronger, just like a seed turning into a flourishing plant. Hold the jar in your hands and say, "As the Moon grows, so do my dreams and desires. I nurture them with love and watch them bloom." Place the jar somewhere you'll see it every day, like your windowsill or bedside table, as a reminder of the growth you're working toward during the waxing moon.

Another great ritual for the waxing Moon is creating a vision board. A vision board is a visual representation of your goals, dreams, and what you want to attract into your life. During the waxing moon, gather some old magazines, scissors, glue, and a piece of poster board or paper. Cut out pictures, words, or phrases that represent your intentions and what you want to manifest. Arrange them on the board in a way that feels inspiring and powerful to you. As you create your vision board, think about how the waxing moon's energy is helping you move closer to these dreams.

After your vision board is complete, place it somewhere you'll see it often. Each time you look at it, you're reminding yourself of your goals and reinforcing the energy of growth and attraction. The waxing Moon will support you in taking steps toward these dreams, helping them become part of your reality.

The waxing moon's energy is also perfect for specific spells that focus on attracting and growing. If you're looking to bring more positivity, creativity, or success into your life, the waxing Moon is the ideal time to cast spells that align with those desires. One simple and effective spell for the waxing Moon is the "Candle of Growth." For this spell, you'll need a green candle (green represents growth and abundance), a small dish of salt, and a pen.

Find a quiet space where you can sit comfortably. Place the green candle on the dish of salt; the salt will help ground and protect your energy during the spell. Take a moment to center yourself with a few deep breaths. Hold the candle in your hands and think about what you want to attract into your life. It could be anything that makes you feel joyful, empowered, or inspired.

Next, use the pen to carve a simple symbol or word that represents your intention into the candle. For example, if you're focusing on creativity, you might carve a small star or the word "Create." As you carve, visualize your intention growing stronger and filling the candle with the energy of the waxing moon.

Light the candle and say, "As the Moon grows, so does my intention. I call upon the waxing moon's power to bring growth, abundance, and joy into my life." Let the candle burn for a few minutes while you focus on your intention. Picture it growing and taking shape, just like the Moon in the sky. When you're ready, blow out the candle and sprinkle a bit of the salt around your space as a way to seal the spell.

Another wonderful spell for the waxing Moon is the "Friendship Circle." This spell is great if you're looking to grow new friendships or strengthen existing ones. For this spell, you'll need a small circle of string or ribbon, a piece of rose quartz (for love and friendship), and a small bowl of water.

Sit in a comfortable spot and place the circle of string on the ground in front of you. Put the rose quartz in the center of the circle and place the bowl of water nearby. Close your eyes and imagine the friends you want to attract or the friendships you want to strengthen. Picture yourself surrounded by supportive, kind, and fun people who make you feel happy and loved.

Dip your fingers into the bowl of water and sprinkle a few drops around the circle, saying, "With this water, I call upon the waxing Moon to help my friendships grow strong and true." Pick up the rose quartz and hold it in your hands, feeling its warm and loving energy. Say, "As the Moon grows, so do my connections. I attract friendships that are joyful, kind, and full of light."

Place the rose quartz somewhere special, like on your windowsill or beside your bed, and keep the string circle as a reminder of the growing friendships you're calling into your life.

The waxing Moon is a time of action, growth, and attraction. When you work with its energy, you're harnessing the natural momentum of the universe to help your intentions and dreams bloom. By practicing rituals, spells, and activities that focus on building up what you desire, you're aligning with the moon's magic and allowing it to support you on your path. Remember, the waxing Moon is your ally, helping you grow and nurture the seeds you've planted in your heart. Whether you're seeking confidence, creativity, friendship, or success, the waxing Moon is there to help your magic flourish and shine. So embrace this phase, take bold steps forward, and watch as your intentions grow alongside the moon's light. The universe is ready to support you, and the waxing Moon is here to guide you on your magical journey.

The Full Moon

The full Moon is one of the most magical and powerful times in the lunar cycle. When the Moon is full, it lights up the night sky with its bright, glowing energy, and you can feel its power buzzing in the air. For witches, this is a time of high energy, celebration, and manifestation. Working with the full Moon allows you to harness its strength to amplify your spells and intentions, making your magic even more potent. The full Moon is a time for both releasing what no longer serves you and embracing the energy needed to manifest your dreams. In this chapter, we'll explore how you can harness the energy of the full moon, create rituals to celebrate this phase, and cast spells that bring your desires to life.

The full Moon occurs roughly every 29 days, halfway through the lunar cycle, when the Moon is completely illuminated by the sun. This is when the moon's energy is at its peak, overflowing with power, which is why it's such an important time for magical work. You might notice that during the full moon, you feel more energetic, emotional, or even restless. That's because the full Moon brings everything to the surface – your hopes, dreams, and even things you might need to let go of. It's like a giant spotlight, revealing everything so you can decide what to embrace and what to release.

One of the best ways to harness the energy of the full Moon is to spend time outside under its light. Simply sitting in the moonlight, closing your eyes, and soaking up its energy can help you feel more connected to the universe and your own magic. Picture the moon's glow filling you up with strength, clarity, and positivity. This is a wonderful time to reflect on your intentions, take stock of how far you've come, and think about what you want to manifest moving forward.

Full Moon energy is all about abundance, clarity, and power. It's perfect for spells that focus on manifesting your dreams, charging your magical tools, or releasing anything that's holding you back. If you've been working on a specific intention since the new moon, the full Moon is when you can celebrate your progress and take it to the next level. Think of it as a checkpoint in your magical journey, where you gather up all the energy you've been building and direct it toward what you truly desire.

Creating a full Moon ritual is a beautiful way to connect with this powerful energy. Rituals don't have to be complicated; they just need to be meaningful to you. One simple full Moon ritual you can try is the "Moonlight Gratitude

Ceremony." This ritual focuses on celebrating the things in your life that you're grateful for, which helps amplify positive energy and open the door for even more blessings to come your way.

To do this ritual, find a quiet place outside where you can see the full moon. If it's too cloudy or you can't go outside, sitting by a window where the moon's light can touch you works just as well. Bring a small piece of paper, a pen, and a candle if you have one. Sit down, take a few deep breaths, and look up at the moon. Let its light wash over you, filling you with a sense of calm and power.

On your piece of paper, write down three things you're grateful for. These can be anything – big or small – that has brought joy, comfort, or growth into your life. It could be a supportive friend, a hobby that makes you happy, or even the way the sun feels on your face in the morning. As you write, let the gratitude fill your heart. When you're finished, hold the paper in your hands, close your eyes, and say, "Under this full moon, I give thanks for the blessings in my life. I open myself to more joy, love, and abundance." If you have a candle, light it now as a symbol of your gratitude glowing brightly.

Another full Moon ritual that many Witches love is the "Full Moon Release Ceremony." This ritual is all about letting go of things that no longer serve you – negative thoughts, bad habits, or anything else that feels heavy and unhelpful. The full moon's light helps you see these things clearly, making it easier to release them and create space for positive energy to flow in.

For this ritual, you'll need a piece of paper, a pen, and a small fireproof container (like a bowl or a cauldron). Find a quiet spot where you won't be disturbed. Under the light of the full moon, write down anything you want to release. This could be fears, worries, or habits you're ready to let go of. Be honest with yourself; the Moon is here to help, not judge. When you're finished, hold the paper in your hands and say, "I release what no longer serves me. Under the light of the full moon, I free myself from these burdens."

Place the paper in the fireproof container and, if it's safe to do so, light the paper with a match or candle. Watch as the paper burns, imagining all the things you're releasing turning into smoke and floating away. As the paper turns to ash, feel the weight lifting off your shoulders. You're now making room for new, positive energy to enter your life.

The full Moon is also the perfect time to cast spells that focus on power and manifestation. Because the full Moon amplifies energy, spells you perform under its light can be especially strong and effective. One spell you might want to try during the full Moon is the "Full Moon Manifestation Spell," designed to help you attract what you truly desire.

For this spell, you'll need a white candle (white symbolizes the Moon and its energy), a small bowl of water, and a silver coin or piece of jewelry. Find a spot where the moonlight can reach you. Sit comfortably, place the candle and bowl of water in front of you, and light the candle. Hold the silver coin in your hands and think about what you want to manifest. It could be a new opportunity, a deeper friendship, or even just more self-love. Picture this desire as clearly as possible, as if it's already part of your life.

When you have a clear image in your mind, say, "Under this full moon, I call upon its power to bring my desires to light. I welcome [state your desire] into my life with open arms." Place the coin into the bowl of water, letting it rest at the bottom. The water represents the moon's influence on emotions and intuition, while the coin symbolizes your intention. Allow the candle to burn for a few minutes as you focus on your desire and feel the moon's energy filling you with confidence and strength.

When you're ready, blow out the candle and leave the bowl of water in a moonlit spot overnight. In the morning, remove the coin and keep it as a charm to remind you of the full moon's magic and your intention. Pour the water onto the ground or into a potted plant, returning it to the Earth with gratitude.

Another powerful spell to try during the full Moon is the "Crystal Charging Spell." Crystals absorb energy, and the full moon's light is perfect for recharging and cleansing them. To charge your crystals, gather the ones you use in your practice, such as rose quartz, amethyst, or clear quartz. Find a spot where the moonlight can touch them, like a windowsill or an outdoor table. Lay the crystals out in a circle, leaving them there overnight.

As you arrange your crystals, say, "Under this full moon's light, I cleanse and charge these stones with energy pure and bright." Picture the moon's glow filling each crystal, clearing away any negativity they may have picked up and infusing them with new, vibrant energy. The next morning, your crystals will be ready to use, charged with the power of the full moon.

Working with the full Moon allows you to harness its abundant, powerful energy for your magical practice. Whether you're performing a gratitude ceremony, a release ritual, or a spell for manifestation, the full moon's light amplifies your intentions and helps bring them to life. By celebrating the full moon, you're connecting with an ancient rhythm that has guided Witches for centuries, tapping into the same magic that has illuminated the night sky for thousands of years. Remember, the full Moon is here to help you release what you no longer need and embrace the power to create the life you desire. So when the Moon is full and glowing brightly, let it light up your path, fill you with its magic, and guide you toward your dreams.

The Waning Moon

After the full Moon shines its brightest, the Moon begins to shrink in the sky. This phase, known as the waning moon, is when the Moon grows smaller each night, moving toward the new Moon and starting the cycle again. For witches, the waning Moon is a time of release, cleansing, and letting go. It's a magical period that encourages you to clear away anything that might be holding you back, whether it's negative energy, bad habits, or old patterns. When you work with the waning moon's energy, you're making space for new beginnings and fresh intentions once the new Moon comes around again. In this chapter, we'll explore the power of the waning moon, how to use its energy for cleansing and releasing, and the best spells to help you let go of what no longer serves you.

The waning Moon phase begins right after the full Moon and continues until the new moon. During this time, the moon's light fades a little more each night, creating a sense of calm and quiet in the world. If the full Moon is about abundance and celebration, the waning Moon is about reflection and release. It's the perfect time to think about the things in your life that might be weighing you down or blocking your path forward. Just as the Moon lets go of its light, this is the time for you to let go of any energy, thoughts, or habits that you don't want to carry with you into the next lunar cycle.

Have you ever felt like something is bothering you, but you're not quite sure what it is? Or maybe you've been holding onto a worry, fear, or habit that you know isn't good for you, but you can't seem to let it go? That's where the magic of the waning Moon comes in. This phase helps you identify what's no longer serving you and supports you in releasing it. By working with the waning moon, you're aligning your magic with nature's rhythm, using its energy to help clear out the old and make room for the new.

One of the most powerful ways to connect with the waning Moon is through releasing and cleansing rituals. These rituals are designed to help you let go of negativity, stress, or anything that's been building up inside you. A simple but effective ritual for the waning Moon is the "Cord Cutting Ceremony." This ritual helps you release any negative attachments or connections that may be draining your energy. It's especially useful if you've been feeling stuck, overwhelmed, or weighed down by a situation or relationship.

To perform the cord-cutting ritual, you'll need a piece of string or ribbon, a pair of scissors, and a quiet space where you won't be disturbed. Sit down and take a few deep breaths to center yourself. Think about the situation, habit, or feeling you want to release. Imagine it as a cord connecting you to something heavy or unwanted. Hold the string in your hands, picturing this cord as a symbol of what you want to let go of. When you feel ready, say, "I release this attachment. It no longer serves me, and I am free." Then, use the scissors to cut the string in half. As you do this, imagine the unwanted energy falling away from you, leaving you lighter and more at peace. Keep the pieces of the string as a reminder that you have the power to let go.

Another great ritual for the waning Moon is a "Cleansing Bath." Water has natural cleansing properties and can help wash away negativity, just like how the moon's light gradually fades during this phase. To create a cleansing bath, fill your bathtub with warm water and add a handful of salt (sea salt or Epsom salt works best) along with a few drops of your favorite essential oil, like lavender or rosemary. If you don't have a bathtub, you can use a basin of water for a foot soak instead.

As you soak in the water, close your eyes and imagine the waning moon's energy flowing through you, carrying away anything that feels heavy, stressful, or unhelpful. Picture all the negativity dissolving into the water, leaving you feeling light, calm, and refreshed. Say to yourself, "I release what no longer serves me. I cleanse my spirit, and

I welcome peace." When you're ready to get out, let the water drain, taking with it all the energy you've released. Pat yourself dry and notice how much lighter you feel.

The waning Moon is also an excellent time for spells that focus on letting go. If there's a habit you want to break, a worry you want to release, or a feeling you need to move past, the energy of the waning Moon will support you. One of the best spells for letting go is the "Banishing Jar Spell." This spell uses the power of the waning Moon to help you banish unwanted habits, thoughts, or energies from your life.

To perform this spell, you'll need a small jar with a lid, a piece of paper, a pen, and some salt. Sit in a quiet place where you can focus on your intention. Think about what you want to banish – it could be a bad habit, a negative thought pattern, or a worry that keeps creeping into your mind. On the piece of paper, write down what you're releasing. Be as specific as you can. For example, you might write, "I release my fear of failure" or "I let go of self-doubt."

Once you've written your intention, fold the paper and place it in the jar. Sprinkle a layer of salt on top of the paper. Salt is known for its purifying properties and will help absorb the energy you're releasing. Close the jar tightly and hold it in your hands. Visualize the waning moon's energy flowing into the jar, surrounding your intention and clearing it away. Say, "As the Moon wanes, so does this energy. I release it and welcome peace and freedom."

Keep the jar somewhere safe until the new moon, when you can bury the paper outside or in a potted plant to complete the cycle of release.

Another spell you might try during the waning Moon is the "Smoke Cleansing Spell." This spell uses the power of herbs to cleanse your space and energy. For this spell, you'll need a bundle of dried herbs, like sage, rosemary, or lavender, and a fireproof bowl or shell. Light the end of the herb bundle and let it smolder, creating smoke. Hold the bowl or shell underneath to catch any ashes.

Gently wave the smoke around yourself, your room, or any objects you want to cleanse. As you do this, imagine the smoke carrying away any negativity, leaving behind only clear, positive energy. Say, "With this smoke, I cleanse and release. I welcome peace and harmony." If you're cleansing a room, make sure to wave the smoke into every corner, as stagnant energy often hides there. When you're finished, extinguish the herb bundle and feel the calmness that the cleansing brings.

The waning Moon reminds us that it's okay to let go. Just as the Moon gradually releases its light, we, too, can release what we no longer need. By using the waning moon's energy for cleansing and banishing, you're making space for new, positive energy to flow into your life. Whether you're performing a simple cord-cutting ritual, soaking in a cleansing bath, or casting a banishing spell, you're taking an important step in your magical practice.

Working with the waning Moon is like a deep, magical breath out. It's a time to reflect on what you've gathered during the full Moon and decide what to keep and what to release. By letting go, you're preparing yourself for the new moon, where you'll have a fresh, open space to plant new intentions. Remember, the waning Moon is your ally in the process of release. It helps you shed the old, stagnant energy so that you can welcome in the new. So, the next time the Moon begins to shrink in the sky, embrace its energy, let go of what's holding you back, and feel the lightness that comes with release. The Moon is here to guide you, showing you that letting go is not an end, but a powerful beginning.

Working with Lunar Cycles

The Moon is always on the move, changing its shape and energy as it journeys through its cycle each month. As a young witch, learning to work with these changes can make your magic even more powerful. The moon's energy affects everything around us—nature, animals, plants, and yes, even us! By understanding the moon's phases and aligning your daily rituals with its energy, you can connect more deeply with your magic and the natural world. In this chapter, we'll explore how to track the moon's journey, create a Moon diary, and work with the moon's energy in your daily life.

One of the most important parts of working with lunar magic is getting to know the moon's phases. The Moon goes through a complete cycle in about 29 days, starting with the new moon, waxing (growing bigger), reaching its peak at the full moon, and then waning (getting smaller) until it becomes a new Moon again. Each of these phases has its own special energy. For example, the new Moon is all about fresh starts and setting intentions, while the full Moon is a time of celebration and manifesting dreams. The waning Moon helps you let go of negativity, and the waxing Moon builds up the energy for growth and attraction. By tracking the moon's journey, you can plan your spells and rituals to align with its power, making them stronger and more effective.

A great way to start working with lunar energy is by simply paying attention to the Moon every day. Take a moment each night to look up at the sky and notice what phase the Moon is in. Is it a thin crescent? Is it half-full, almost full, or a bright, glowing orb? By observing the Moon regularly, you'll begin to feel more in tune with its changes. You might even start noticing how different Moon phases affect your energy and mood. For instance, during the full moon, you might feel more energized or emotional, while the waning Moon could make you feel calmer and more introspective.

A fun and helpful tool for tracking the moon's journey is a Moon phase calendar. You can find these calendars online, in witchy books, or even make one yourself. A Moon phase calendar shows you the dates of each Moon phase throughout the month, so you know exactly when the new moon, full moon, waxing, and waning moons will occur. Hang it up in your room or keep it in your book of shadows to remind you of the moon's cycles.

Another fantastic way to deepen your connection with the Moon is to create a Moon diary. A Moon diary is like a magical journal where you keep track of the moon's phases and how they affect you. This is a wonderful practice that helps you tune into the moon's energy and understand how it influences your daily life. Each night, take a few minutes to jot down your observations about the Moon and how you're feeling. Were you feeling extra creative today? Did you feel calm, restless, or maybe a little emotional? Write it all down.

You can also include any dreams you had, any spells or rituals you performed, and how they turned out. Over time, you'll start to notice patterns. For example, you might find that you have vivid dreams around the full Moon or that you feel more focused during the waxing moon. Noticing these patterns helps you understand how to work with the moon's energy more effectively in your magical practice.

Here's how you can start your own Moon diary: Find a notebook or journal that you love. It can be simple or fancy, whatever feels right for you. Each night, write down the date and note the moon's phase. Then, write about your day—how you felt, any interesting events, and your thoughts. If you performed a spell or ritual, describe what you did and how it went. If you have a Moon phase calendar, you can use it to mark the different phases in your diary, so you always know where the Moon is in its cycle.

Your Moon diary is your personal record of how the moon's energy affects you and your magic. There's no right or wrong way to keep a Moon diary; the most important thing is to be honest and open with yourself. Over time, this practice will help you understand your own rhythms and how to harness the moon's power in your daily life.

Once you've started tracking the Moon and keeping a Moon diary, you can begin to align your daily rituals with the moon's energy. Every day is an opportunity to work a little bit of Moon magic into your life. Simple daily rituals, like setting intentions in the morning or practicing gratitude at night, can help you stay connected to the Moon and its phases. These rituals don't have to be complicated; they just need to feel meaningful to you.

For example, when the Moon is waxing (growing bigger in the sky), it's a great time to focus on growth and attraction. During the waxing moon, you might create a daily ritual of saying positive affirmations to attract what you want into your life. In the morning, stand in front of a mirror, look yourself in the eyes, and say an affirmation like, "I am confident and growing every day." Repeat it three times, letting the words sink in. This simple ritual aligns with the waxing moon's energy, helping you build up your confidence and self-belief.

During the full moon, you can create a daily ritual of celebrating your accomplishments. The full Moon is a time of abundance and manifestation, so it's the perfect time to recognize what you've achieved. Each night during the full Moon phase, take a moment to write down one thing you're proud of or grateful for. Light a candle and say, "I celebrate the abundance in my life. I welcome joy and success." This ritual not only connects you with the full moon's energy but also fills your heart with gratitude and positivity.

When the Moon is waning (shrinking in the sky), focus on release and cleansing. A lovely daily ritual during the waning Moon is the "Release and Clear" ritual. Before bed, sit quietly, close your eyes, and take a few deep breaths. Think about anything that felt heavy or stressful during the day. Imagine the waning moon's energy washing over you, gently taking away those worries. Say to yourself, "I release what no longer serves me. I make space for peace and clarity." Visualize the negative energy dissolving, leaving you feeling calm and light. This ritual helps you let go of negativity and prepare for a restful sleep.

For the new moon, your daily ritual can be about setting intentions and planting seeds for the month ahead. In the morning, light a candle or hold a crystal in your hands and think about what you want to bring into your life. Say, "I set my intention to welcome [state your goal] into my life." You can also write your intention on a piece of paper and place it on your altar or under your pillow. This ritual aligns with the new moon's energy of new beginnings and helps you focus on your goals with a clear, fresh mindset.

You can also use daily Moon magic in small, simple ways. For example, drink a cup of tea while gazing at the moon, whispering your dreams to the stars, or placing a crystal on your windowsill to soak up the moon's energy. Even just taking a moment to look at the Moon each night and thank it for its guidance can be a powerful daily ritual that keeps you connected to your magic.

Working with lunar cycles in your daily life is all about tuning into the moon's energy and using it to support your intentions, growth, and well-being. By tracking the moon's journey, keeping a Moon diary, and practicing daily rituals aligned with the moon's phases, you're building a deeper relationship with the natural world and your inner magic. Remember, the Moon is always there, changing and flowing, just like you. When you work with its cycles, you're embracing the rhythms of nature and using them to navigate your path as a witch.

As you continue to explore Moon magic, you'll find that the Moon is a constant companion, lighting up your path and helping you harness the power within you. Your daily rituals, guided by the moon's energy, will become a source of strength, joy, and inspiration. So take out your Moon diary, look up at the sky, and let the moon's light fill you with its magic. The more you work with the moon, the more you'll discover how its cycles can guide you, support you, and help you grow as a young witch. Trust in the moon's wisdom and let it be your guide on this magical journey.

Monthly Lunar Magic

T he Moon is a constant companion in the sky, guiding us through its phases every month. Each phase holds a unique energy, and as a young witch, learning how to use this energy in your magical practice can make a big difference. Monthly lunar magic is all about planning your spells, rituals, and intentions according to the moon's cycle, and it's easier than you might think. The key is to tune into the moon's rhythm and align your magic with its natural flow. In this chapter, we'll explore how to plan spells based on the moon's phases, how to prepare for the new and full moons, and how to use monthly Moon meditations to deepen your connection with lunar energy.

The Moon goes through a full cycle in about 29 days, starting with the new moon, waxing (growing larger), reaching its peak at the full moon, and then waning (shrinking) until it becomes a new Moon again. Each part of this cycle brings a different kind of energy, which can support different types of magic. When you plan your spells around the moon's phases, you're working with the natural flow of energy, which helps make your magic stronger and more effective.

The cycle begins with the **new Moon**, which is all about new beginnings, setting intentions, and planting seeds for the future. This is the perfect time to do spells for anything you want to attract or start in your life. For example, if you're looking to start a new hobby, make new friends, or set a goal, the new moon's energy will support your efforts. Think of the new Moon as a blank canvas; it's a time to dream, wish, and plan. Your magic during the new Moon is like planting seeds in a garden. It may take time for those seeds to grow, but by setting your intentions now, you're giving them the best chance to flourish.

As the Moon begins to wax (grow larger), its energy increases. The waxing Moon is about building up, growing stronger, and attracting what you want into your life. Spells for growth, abundance, and attracting positive things are perfect during this phase. If you've set an intention to become more confident, the waxing Moon is the time to nurture that intention. You might perform spells that focus on self-love, courage, or improving your skills. The waxing moon's energy helps you take action and make progress toward your goals.

When the Moon reaches its full phase, its energy is at its peak. The **full Moon** is a time of celebration, manifestation, and abundance. This is when you can see the results of the intentions you set during the new moon. If you've been working on a goal, the full Moon is a wonderful time to acknowledge your progress and give your intentions an extra boost of energy. It's also the perfect time for spells that focus on manifesting your dreams, charging your magical tools (like crystals and talismans), and releasing anything that's been holding you back. The full Moon lights up the night sky, and its energy can light up your path, showing you what's possible.

After the full moon, the Moon starts to wane (grow smaller). The **waning Moon** is all about release, letting go, and clearing out anything that's no longer serving you. This is the time for spells that focus on banishing negativity, breaking bad habits, or clearing your space of unwanted energy. The waning moon's energy supports you in shedding the old so that you can make room for new growth when the cycle begins again with the next new moon.

Planning your spells according to the moon's phases can be as simple or as detailed as you like. Some Witches like to create a monthly "lunar spell calendar," where they plan out their spells and rituals based on the moon's cycle. You can make your own lunar spell calendar using a notebook or a calendar app. Mark the dates of the new moon, full moon, and key waxing and waning phases. Then, write down what kind of spells or rituals you'd like to do during each phase. This helps you stay organized and ensures that you're working with the moon's energy in a way that supports your intentions.

As part of your monthly lunar magic, it's important to prepare for the new and full moons, as these are the most powerful points in the lunar cycle. The new Moon is your opportunity to set new intentions and plant the seeds for what you want to grow in the coming month. To prepare for the new moon, take some time to reflect on what you want to bring into your life. Sit quietly with a journal or a piece of paper and ask yourself: What do I want to start? What do I want to attract? What changes do I want to make? Write down your thoughts, wishes, and goals. This helps you get clear on your intentions and gives your magic a strong foundation.

Once you have your intentions, create a simple new Moon ritual to set them in motion. You might light a candle, hold a crystal, or write your intentions on a piece of paper and place it under the moonlight. Say your intentions out loud, giving them power and sending them out into the universe. For example, you might say, "I set my intention to welcome more joy into my life." This ritual doesn't have to be long or complicated; it's all about focusing your energy and starting the cycle with a clear purpose.

The full Moon is another important time for monthly lunar magic. Preparing for the full Moon involves gathering what you need for any spells or rituals you want to perform. This might include candles, crystals, herbs, or your magical tools. The full Moon is also a great time to charge your tools by placing them outside or on a windowsill where they can soak up the moon's energy. Before the full moon, take some time to think about what you want to manifest and what you're ready to release. The full moon's energy can help you amplify your desires and let go of anything that's blocking your path.

One of the most powerful ways to work with the moon's energy each month is through Moon meditation. Meditation is a practice that helps you connect with your inner self and the universe. During the moon's cycle, meditating can help you tune into its energy and use it to support your intentions. You can do a Moon meditation at any time during the month, but it's especially helpful during the new moon, full moon, and key waxing and waning phases.

A new Moon meditation is all about focusing on your intentions and planting the seeds for your dreams. To do this meditation, find a quiet place where you won't be disturbed. Sit comfortably, close your eyes, and take a few deep breaths to calm your mind. Picture the new Moon in the sky, dark and mysterious, holding endless possibilities. As you breathe, imagine your intentions as tiny seeds in your heart. With each breath, feel these seeds growing stronger, ready to take root in the universe. Visualize your intentions blossoming into reality, just like seeds growing into beautiful flowers. Hold onto this image for a few minutes, then gently open your eyes and carry that energy with you into the rest of the month.

A full Moon meditation, on the other hand, is about celebrating your progress and releasing what no longer serves you. For this meditation, sit in a place where you can see the full moon, if possible. Close your eyes and imagine the moon's light filling you up, shining on all your accomplishments and dreams. Feel its energy surrounding you, making you feel strong and empowered. Then, think about anything you're ready to let go of—fears, worries, habits, or negative energy. Picture the moon's light gently pulling these things away, like waves washing away sand on the shore. As you breathe, feel yourself becoming lighter and more free, open to the new possibilities that the moon's energy brings.

Monthly Moon meditations help you stay connected to the moon's phases and your own inner magic. By taking time to reflect, set intentions, and release energy throughout the moon's cycle, you're working in harmony with the universe and strengthening your practice as a witch.

Working with monthly lunar magic is all about using the moon's energy to support your intentions, goals, and personal growth. By planning your spells according to the lunar cycle, preparing for the new and full moons, and practicing Moon meditation, you're creating a magical routine that aligns with the natural world. The Moon is always there, guiding you through its phases and showing you when to plant, grow, celebrate, and release. When you embrace this rhythm, you'll find that your magic flows more easily and that your intentions become reality with the moon's guidance. So, take out your lunar spell calendar, prepare for the new and full moons, and let the moonlight inspire your monthly magic. The Moon is here to be your ally, shining its light on your path as you navigate your journey as a young witch.

YEARLY MOON MAGIC

As a young witch, you may already know that the Moon holds special power, guiding us through its phases every month. But did you know that the Moon also has a unique influence throughout the entire year? Yearly Moon magic is about understanding special Moon events like blue moons, celebrating lunar sabbats (special Moon celebrations), and creating a yearly lunar plan to align your magical practices with the cycles of nature. By learning to work with the moon's energy over the course of the year, you can enhance your spells and rituals, making them more meaningful and effective. Let's explore how to connect with the moon's yearly rhythm to harness its full magical potential.

Every year, the Moon goes through its cycle of phases roughly 12 times, creating what we call the "lunar calendar." Each month, the Moon follows its familiar pattern of waxing (growing bigger), becoming full, waning (getting smaller), and disappearing into the new moon. But sometimes, something extraordinary happens—an extra full Moon appears in a month. This special event is called a "blue moon."

A blue Moon is a rare occurrence, happening roughly once every two to three years. There are two kinds of blue moons. The first type is when there are two full moons in a single calendar month. The second type is when there are four full moons in one season instead of the usual three. Because they are so rare, blue moons are seen as a time of extra magic, power, and opportunity. You might have heard the phrase "once in a blue moon," which means something special or uncommon—exactly what a blue Moon is in the world of witchcraft!

When a blue Moon comes around, it's the perfect time to focus on your deepest wishes, dreams, and desires. The energy of a blue Moon is like the moon's magic doubled; it provides you with a unique chance to work on big, important spells or intentions. For example, if there's something you've been hoping to manifest for a long time, like a major life change, a blue Moon is an excellent time to put all your energy into making that dream a reality. Because blue moons don't happen often, they remind us that magic is both special and powerful, especially when we take the time to truly focus on our desires.

During a blue moon, you might want to perform a "Wish Jar Spell." To do this, gather a small jar, some paper, a pen, and a few items that represent your wish, like small crystals, herbs, or charms. Write your deepest wish on a piece of paper, fold it up, and place it in the jar. Add your crystals, herbs, or charms to the jar, filling it with your magical energy and intention. Hold the jar in your hands, close your eyes, and imagine your wish coming true. Say, "Under this blue moon, I set my wish free. With this magic, it comes back to me." Seal the jar and place it somewhere special. Each time you see the jar, let it remind you of the blue moon's magic and the power of your intention.

Another exciting part of yearly Moon magic is celebrating the lunar sabbats. In witchcraft, sabbats are seasonal celebrations that honor nature's cycles and the changing of the seasons. While many Witches celebrate the solar sabbats, which follow the sun's path, there are also lunar sabbats that focus on the moon's energy throughout the year. Celebrating these lunar sabbats can help you feel more in sync with the Moon and deepen your connection to the magic around you.

There are four main lunar sabbats that correspond with the four seasons: Imbolc (early spring), Beltane (spring into summer), Lammas or Lughnasadh (late summer), and Samhain (late autumn). Each lunar sabbat has its own magical energy and themes, which you can honor through rituals, spells, and celebrations. These sabbats are perfect opportunities to reflect on how the moon's energy changes throughout the year and how you can use that energy in your practice.

Imbolc, celebrated in early February, marks the beginning of spring. It's a time of new beginnings, hope, and light returning to the world. The moon's energy during Imbolc is fresh and filled with potential, much like the first stirrings of plants growing beneath the earth. During Imbolc, you can perform spells for growth, renewal, and creativity. One lovely ritual to celebrate the Moon at Imbolc is to light a white candle (representing the Moon and the coming light) and say, "As the Moon grows, so does my strength and creativity."

Beltane, celebrated in early May, marks the height of spring and the approach of summer. The moon's energy at Beltane is vibrant, full of life, and overflowing with abundance. This is a time for spells of love, joy, and celebration. To honor the Moon at Beltane, you can create a "Flower Moon Charm." Gather some fresh flowers, a ribbon, and a small stone. Arrange the flowers into a small bundle, tie them together with the ribbon, and attach the stone. Hold the bundle under the moonlight and say, "Moon of Beltane, bless this charm with love, joy, and abundance."

Lammas (or Lughnasadh) is celebrated in early August and marks the beginning of the harvest season. The moon's energy during Lammas is about abundance, gratitude, and reflection. It's a time to give thanks for what the year has brought and to gather the "harvest" of your efforts. During Lammas, you might perform a spell for gratitude or abundance, such as creating a gratitude jar filled with notes of what you're thankful for.

Samhain, celebrated at the end of October, is the final lunar sabbat of the year. The moon's energy during Samhain is mystical, introspective, and deeply connected to the spirit world. This is a time for spells of protection, honoring ancestors, and reflection. During Samhain, you can honor the Moon by lighting a candle and remembering those who have come before you. Say, "Under this Moon of Samhain, I honor the past and welcome the future."

Along with celebrating blue moons and lunar sabbats, one of the most powerful ways to work with yearly Moon magic is to create a yearly lunar plan. A yearly lunar plan is like a magical roadmap that outlines how you want to work with the moon's energy throughout the year. It helps you stay organized, set long-term intentions, and make the most of the moon's changing energy.

To create your yearly lunar plan, start by getting a calendar or planner. Mark the dates of each new moon, full moon, and blue moon. Then, add the lunar sabbats—Imbolc, Beltane, Lammas, and Samhain—so you know when each seasonal celebration is coming up. Once you have all the Moon events on your calendar, think about what kind of magic you want to focus on during each part of the year.

For example, during the new moons in spring, you might set intentions for growth, creativity, and new projects. During the full moons in summer, you can focus on abundance, joy, and celebration. The waning moons in autumn are perfect for releasing, reflecting, and preparing for the quieter months ahead. When the blue Moon arrives, you might choose to work on a special, long-term goal that you've been dreaming about.

In your yearly lunar plan, jot down ideas for spells, rituals, and activities you want to do during each Moon phase and sabbat. You might write, "New Moon in March: set intention for confidence," or "Full Moon in July: perform a gratitude ritual." Having a plan helps you stay focused and connected to the moon's energy, making your magical practice feel more structured and intentional.

Your yearly lunar plan doesn't have to be set in stone. The beauty of working with the Moon is that its energy, like life, is always changing. Feel free to adjust your plan as you go, adding or changing spells and rituals based on how you're feeling and what you need. The most important thing is to use the plan as a guide to help you align your magic with the moon's cycle over the year.

Yearly Moon magic is a powerful way to deepen your connection with the Moon and the natural world. By understanding blue moons, celebrating lunar sabbats, and creating a yearly lunar plan, you're embracing the moon's influence not just month by month, but throughout the entire year. This allows you to use its energy in a way that supports your growth, dreams, and magical journey.

Remember, the Moon is always there to guide you, lighting up your path with its silver glow. As you work with its energy over the year, you'll find that your spells become more effective, your intentions clearer, and your connection to magic stronger. So take out your calendar, mark those special Moon dates, and let the moon's magic be your guide through the seasons. Whether you're celebrating a blue moon, performing a ritual at a lunar sabbat, or following your yearly lunar plan, the moon's energy will support you every step of the way. Your journey as a Witch is just beginning, and the Moon is here to light it up with its endless magic.

Moon Water

and Other Lunar Tools

The Moon holds a magical energy that can help amplify your spells, rituals, and daily life. One of the easiest and most effective ways to harness this power is by making Moon water. Moon water is exactly what it sounds like: water that has been charged with the energy of the moon. This simple, yet powerful magical tool has been used by Witches for centuries to bring the moon's energy into their practices. It's versatile, easy to make, and can be used in many different ways. In this chapter, you'll learn what Moon water is, how to make it, and the many magical ways you can use it in your spells and rituals.

So, what is Moon water, and why is it so special? Moon water is simply water that has been left out under the light of the Moon to soak up its energy. Just like the Moon influences the tides and the natural world, it also affects the water you leave out to charge. When you make Moon water, you're capturing the moon's power and bringing it into a form that you can use whenever you need it. The great thing about Moon water is that it carries the energy of the specific Moon phase when it was created. This means you can make different types of Moon water depending on the moon's phase, and each one will have a slightly different energy to work with in your spells.

For example, Moon water made during the full Moon is perfect for spells of abundance, empowerment, and manifesting dreams. It's full of the moon's peak energy, which can help you bring your desires to life. On the other hand, Moon water made during the new Moon is great for setting intentions, starting new projects, and planting the seeds of your dreams. New Moon water carries the energy of beginnings and potential. You can even make Moon water during a blue Moon (a rare event when two full moons occur in one month) for extra magical power, as blue Moon water is known to amplify spells and intentions in a big way.

Now that you know what Moon water is, let's talk about how to make it. Creating Moon water is simple and requires just a few supplies. You'll need a jar or glass container with a lid, some clean water (tap water, spring water, or even rainwater works), and a safe place where the moonlight can reach your container. If you have crystals like clear quartz or moonstone, you can add them to your jar for an extra boost of energy, but this step is optional.

To make Moon water, start by choosing a night when the Moon is in a phase that matches the energy you want to capture. For example, if you're looking to create Moon water for manifesting dreams, the full Moon is the best time. If you're setting new intentions, use the new moon. Once you've picked the perfect night, fill your jar with water. You can also place a small crystal inside the jar if you like. Before sealing the jar, hold it in your hands and take a moment to set your intention. Close your eyes and say, "I charge this water with the power of the moon. May it be filled with energy, light, and magic."

Next, place the jar outside or on a windowsill where it will be bathed in moonlight. Leave the water out overnight to soak up the moon's energy. If you're making Moon water during the new moon, don't worry if the Moon isn't visible; the energy of the new Moon is still present and will charge the water just the same. In the morning, bring your jar inside and seal it with a lid. Your Moon water is now ready to use!

There are many ways you can use your Moon water in your magical practice. One of the most popular uses is for cleansing. Moon water is perfect for clearing away negative energy and creating a fresh, positive atmosphere. You can sprinkle a little Moon water around your room or sacred space to cleanse it of any unwanted energy. If you have magical tools, like crystals, tarot cards, or amulets, you can cleanse them by gently wiping them with a cloth dipped in Moon water. This helps clear away any negative vibes they might have picked up and fills them with fresh, moon-charged energy.

You can also use Moon water in your spells and rituals. For example, if you're doing a spell to attract love, success, or confidence, sprinkle a few drops of Moon water onto your candles, crystals, or spell jar to enhance its power. The water carries the energy of the Moon phase it was made under, adding an extra layer of magic to your work. If you're doing a self-care ritual, like taking a bath or meditating, add a splash of Moon water to the bath or dab a few drops on your wrists to surround yourself with the moon's soothing energy.

Another way to use Moon water is in your beauty and self-care routines. You can add a little Moon water to your skincare products, like face mist or body lotion, to charge them with positive energy. When you apply them, you're not just taking care of your skin—you're also bringing the moon's magic into your daily routine. For an extra magical touch, you can say an affirmation as you use these products, like, "I am glowing with the light of the moon."

You can also drink Moon water, but only if you've used a clean, sealed container and safe, drinkable water. Drinking Moon water can help you connect with the moon's energy from the inside out. Before taking a sip, hold the jar in your hands and take a moment to think about what you want to invite into your life. As you drink, imagine the moon's light filling you with its power and positivity. This is especially wonderful to do during the full Moon when the moon's energy is at its peak.

Another fun way to use Moon water is in your plant care routine. Plants love Moon water because it carries the nourishing energy of nature. You can use Moon water to water your plants, helping them grow strong and healthy. As you pour the water into the soil, imagine your plants soaking up the moon's magic. You can say a little blessing, like, "May you grow with the strength of the moon." This is a great way to share the moon's energy with your plant friends and create a magical environment in your space.

You can also use Moon water for drawing symbols or sigils. If you're working on a spell or intention, use a small brush or your finger dipped in Moon water to draw symbols on your skin, candles, or paper. This adds a magical boost to your work, as the Moon water acts like a magical ink charged with lunar power. For example, you might draw a heart symbol on your wrist for love, or a star on a candle to enhance a spell for success.

Making Moon water is a simple, magical way to bring the moon's energy into your everyday life. The best part is that you can create Moon water whenever you need it and use it in countless ways. Whether you're cleansing your space, enhancing a spell, nurturing your plants, or sipping it for an extra dose of lunar magic, Moon water is a versatile tool that every Witch can benefit from. Just remember to set your intention when making your Moon water, so it's filled with the specific energy you want to work with.

As you continue to explore Moon magic, you'll find that Moon water becomes a treasured part of your practice. It's like having a little bit of the moon's magic right at your fingertips, ready to use whenever you need it. Experiment with making Moon water during different phases and notice how each one feels. You might find that full Moon water makes you feel powerful and confident, while new Moon water feels calming and full of potential.

The Moon offers its light and energy to us freely, and making Moon water is a beautiful way to capture that gift and use it to enhance our lives. So the next time the Moon is shining in the sky, grab a jar, set out some water, and let the Moon fill it with its magic. You'll have a versatile tool to use in your spells, rituals, and daily routines, helping you stay connected to the moon's power and your own inner magic. Embrace the moon's energy, experiment with different ways to use your Moon water, and watch as your magical practice grows stronger with each lunar cycle.

LUNAR CRYSTALS

C rystals are powerful tools in witchcraft, each with its own unique energy that can help you in your magical practice. Some crystals are closely linked to the moon, carrying its calming, intuitive, and transformative energy. Using lunar crystals in your spells and rituals can help you connect more deeply with the moon's magic. In this chapter, you'll learn about the crystals most associated with the moon, how to charge them under moonlight, and how to use them in your spells. These crystals can become your magical companions, guiding you through the lunar cycle and enhancing your power as a young witch.

Certain crystals are known for their connection to the moon, each resonating with different aspects of lunar energy. Moonstone is one of the most famous lunar crystals. It comes in beautiful, shimmering colors, often with a bluish or white glow that looks like moonlight captured in stone. Moonstone is linked to intuition, dreams, and the natural rhythms of life. It's like a little piece of the Moon you can carry with you. If you're looking to strengthen your intuition, work with your emotions, or connect more deeply with the moon, moonstone is the perfect crystal to have in your magical toolkit.

Another wonderful lunar crystal is selenite. Named after Selene, the Greek goddess of the moon, selenite has a translucent, milky appearance, often forming in long, delicate sheets or wands. This crystal is known for its calming, cleansing energy. It's great for clearing away negative vibes, creating a peaceful atmosphere, and helping you connect with your higher self. Selenite is often used to cleanse other crystals, too, making it a versatile tool in your magical practice. It doesn't need to be charged often and is especially effective when used in Moon rituals.

Labradorite is another crystal associated with lunar energy. It has a mystical appearance, with flashes of color that look like the northern lights. Labradorite is known for its ability to boost psychic abilities, protect your aura, and enhance magical work. If you're working on spells that involve intuition, dream magic, or protection, labradorite is a fantastic crystal to use. Its shimmering surface reminds you of the moon's transformative power and its ability to illuminate hidden truths.

Amethyst, while not strictly a lunar crystal, is also connected to the moon's energy. Its soothing purple color resonates with the moon's calming influence and is often used for dream work, meditation, and enhancing spiritual awareness. Amethyst can help you clear your mind, calm your emotions, and open up to the wisdom of the moon. It's a wonderful crystal for new Witches who want to explore their intuition and connect with their inner selves.

Once you have your lunar crystals, it's important to charge them under the moonlight. Charging crystals means allowing them to absorb energy from the moon, which enhances their natural properties and fills them with magical power. The best time to charge your crystals is during the full Moon when the moon's energy is at its peak. However, you can charge them during any Moon phase to capture the specific energy you want to work with. For example, charging crystals during the new Moon will fill them with energy for new beginnings, while charging them during the waxing Moon is great for growth and attraction.

To charge your crystals, choose a night when the Moon is visible and find a spot where the moonlight can reach them. This could be a windowsill, a balcony, or a safe outdoor space. Before placing your crystals outside, hold them in your hands and take a moment to set your intention. Close your eyes and imagine the moon's light filling each crystal, infusing it with its power and energy. You might say something like, "I charge these crystals with the light of the moon. May they be filled with magic and strength."

Place the crystals in a small dish or directly on a surface where they won't be disturbed. Leave them out overnight to soak up the moon's energy. If you're worried about them getting wet or damaged, you can cover them with a clear glass or place them inside by a window where the moonlight can reach them. In the morning, bring your crystals inside. They are now charged and ready to use in your magical practice!

Incorporating moon-charged crystals into your spells and rituals is a powerful way to harness lunar energy. One simple way to use your crystals is to hold them during meditation or spell work to amplify your intention. For example, if you're working on a spell for self-love and confidence, hold a moonstone in your hands as you focus on your intention. Feel the crystal's energy merging with yours, boosting your inner strength and helping you connect with the moon's loving, nurturing power.

You can also place crystals on your altar to enhance the energy of your magical space. Create a small Moon altar using moonstone, selenite, and labradorite to represent the moon's different aspects. Arrange them in a circle with a candle in the center. Light the candle during your spells or rituals to invoke the moon's energy and create a space that feels calm, sacred, and filled with magic. Adding crystals to your altar helps you stay connected to the moon's cycles and brings a sense of peace and focus to your magical work.

Another way to use Moon crystals in your spells is to create crystal-infused Moon water. After charging your crystals under the moon, place them in a jar of water and leave it out in the moonlight to create Moon water charged with crystal energy. This is especially powerful when using moonstone or selenite, as their energies blend beautifully with the moon's light. You can then use this crystal-infused Moon water for cleansing, anointing candles, or even adding a splash to your bath for a magical self-care ritual.

If you're working on spells for protection, intuition, or dream magic, consider placing a piece of labradorite or amethyst under your pillow at night. This helps you connect with the moon's energy while you sleep, enhancing your dreams and providing psychic protection. As you place the crystal under your pillow, say a little blessing like, "Moonlight, guide my dreams and keep me safe in your light." This simple ritual can bring calm, insightful dreams and help you feel connected to the Moon even while you rest.

When doing spells for releasing and letting go during the waning moon, you can use selenite as a cleansing tool. Hold the selenite in your hand and gently wave it around your body, imagining it sweeping away any negative energy, doubts, or worries. Feel the moon's energy working through the crystal, clearing away anything that no longer serves you. Afterward, place the selenite on your altar or in a safe spot to continue radiating its calming, cleansing energy throughout your space.

Creating a crystal grid is another powerful way to incorporate Moon crystals into your magic. A crystal grid is a pattern of crystals arranged with a specific intention in mind. To create a moon-inspired grid, gather your Moon crystals (moonstone, selenite, labradorite, amethyst) and place them in a circular pattern, with a larger crystal or candle in the center to act as the focus point. You can create grids for different intentions, such as "manifesting dreams," "protection," or "emotional healing," depending on what you want to work on. As you arrange the crystals, focus on your intention and visualize the moon's light flowing through the grid, activating its energy.

Remember to cleanse and recharge your crystals regularly, especially if you use them often in your spells and rituals. The moon's energy naturally cleanses and revitalizes crystals, so placing them under the moonlight every month is a wonderful way to keep their energy fresh and powerful. If a crystal ever feels heavy or dull, it's a sign that it needs a recharge. Let the moonlight work its magic, filling your crystals with its calming, intuitive power.

Lunar crystals are like tiny pieces of the moon's magic that you can carry with you wherever you go. They connect you to the moon's energy, enhance your spells, and help you navigate your magical path with confidence and clarity. By learning how to work with moonstone, selenite, labradorite, and amethyst, you're adding powerful tools to your witch's toolkit, tools that can guide you through the moon's cycles and support you in every phase of your journey. So, the next time the Moon is shining in the sky, gather your crystals, set them out under its light, and let the Moon fill them with its magic. Your lunar crystals are now ready to help you manifest, cleanse, and grow in your practice as a young witch.

Lunar Symbols
and Charms

S ymbols have been a key part of magic and witchcraft for centuries, serving as visual reminders of the energies we wish to call upon. The moon, with its mysterious glow and ever-changing phases, has inspired many symbols that can enhance your magical practice. These lunar symbols capture the moon's energy, helping you connect with its power in your spells, rituals, and daily life. From simple crescent shapes to complex talismans, lunar symbols and charms can be incredibly helpful as you navigate your path as a young witch. In this chapter, we'll explore the different symbols associated with the moon, how to create a Moon talisman, and how to use lunar symbols in your witchcraft.

The Moon has been represented by various symbols throughout history, each reflecting its unique energy and phases. One of the most common and powerful symbols is the crescent moon. This shape, resembling a thin slice of the moon, is linked to new beginnings, growth, and the waxing Moon phase when the Moon grows larger each night. The crescent Moon can also symbolize the goddess energy that many Witches associate with the moon, embodying qualities like intuition, creativity, and emotional strength. When you draw or wear a crescent Moon symbol, you're calling on the moon's energy to help you grow, create, and connect with your inner wisdom.

Another important lunar symbol is the full moon, which represents abundance, clarity, and the peak of power. In magical practices, the full Moon is a time for celebrating successes, manifesting dreams, and releasing what no longer serves you. The full Moon symbol is often drawn as a circle, representing completeness and the culmination of the lunar cycle. When you use this symbol in your spells or wear it as jewelry, you're tapping into the full moon's energy to amplify your intentions and make your magic stronger. The circle of the full Moon also reminds you that life is a cycle, constantly moving through phases of growth, harvest, and release.

The triple Moon symbol is another popular representation of the moon's energy. It shows three phases of the moon: the waxing crescent, the full moon, and the waning crescent. This symbol represents the different aspects of the moon's cycle and is often associated with the "triple goddess" in witchcraft, embodying the energies of growth, power, and release. The triple Moon reminds you that the Moon is always changing, just like life, and that each phase has its own magic to offer. When you draw or use the triple Moon in your practice, you're connecting with the moon's full cycle and honoring all aspects of its power.

Now that you know some of the key symbols of the Moon in magic, let's explore how to create your own Moon talisman. A talisman is a charm or object that carries magical energy and is used to bring luck, protection, or specific qualities into your life. A Moon talisman can help you carry the moon's energy with you, offering guidance and support as you go about your day. Creating a Moon talisman is a personal and magical process that lets you infuse the object with your own intentions and the moon's power.

To create a Moon talisman, you'll need a small, flat object that you can draw or carve on. This could be a piece of jewelry, a stone, a wooden disk, or even a piece of clay that you shape yourself. If you prefer, you can also use a small charm or pendant that already has a crescent or full Moon shape. The most important part is that this object feels special to you and is something you'll enjoy using or wearing.

Begin by deciding what energy or intention you want your Moon talisman to carry. Do you want it to bring you confidence and courage? Help you connect with your intuition? Or perhaps protect you as you explore your magical path? Once you have a clear intention in mind, hold the object in your hands and close your eyes. Take a few deep breaths, imagining the moon's light filling the talisman, infusing it with your chosen intention. You might say a small incantation, such as, "I charge this talisman with the moon's power. May it guide me, protect me, and fill my path with light."

Next, draw or carve a lunar symbol onto the surface of your talisman. If you're using a stone or disk, you can use a marker, paint, or a carving tool to add the symbol. You might choose a crescent Moon for growth and new beginnings, a full Moon for power and manifestation, or the triple Moon for balance and intuition. If you're using a charm or pendant that already has a Moon shape, you can simply hold it and visualize the moon's energy filling it with magic.

After you've created your talisman, it's time to charge it under the moonlight. Place the talisman outside or on a windowsill where it can soak up the moon's energy. The best time to do this is during a phase that matches your intention. For example, if you made a talisman for new beginnings, charge it under the new moon. If it's for strength and courage, the full Moon is ideal. Leave it out overnight, allowing the Moon to fill it with its power.

The next morning, your Moon talisman will be ready to use! You can carry it in your pocket, wear it as a necklace, or place it on your altar as a reminder of your intention and the moon's support. Each time you hold or see your talisman, remember the energy you infused into it and let it guide you. Talismans are wonderful tools for helping you stay connected to the moon's magic and your own inner power.

Lunar symbols can also be used in your witchcraft practice in many other ways. You can draw them on candles, spell jars, or pieces of paper to focus your intentions. For example, if you're doing a spell to attract confidence, draw a crescent Moon on your candle or spell jar to invite the moon's energy of growth and empowerment. As the candle burns or the spell jar sits on your altar, the lunar symbol will enhance your magic, aligning it with the moon's power.

Another way to use lunar symbols is in your daily rituals. For instance, you might draw a small crescent Moon on your wrist with a washable marker to remind yourself to stay open to new opportunities throughout the day. Or, if you're feeling a bit scattered or anxious, draw a circle (the full Moon symbol) on a piece of paper and place it under your pillow at night. This simple act invites the full moon's energy of calmness and clarity into your dreams, helping you wake up feeling centered and focused.

If you like working with crystals, try combining lunar symbols with your crystal magic. Place a piece of moonstone or selenite on top of a paper where you've drawn a crescent or full moon. This creates a powerful combination of lunar energy that you can use to charge your crystals, spell ingredients, or even your Moon water. The symbols act like a beacon, drawing in the moon's magic and infusing it into whatever you're working with.

When performing rituals during the different Moon phases, consider incorporating lunar symbols into your circle casting. Use your finger, a wand, or a small stick to draw a crescent, full moon, or triple Moon symbol on the ground as you cast your circle. This adds an extra layer of lunar energy to your ritual space, protecting it and filling it with the moon's guidance. As you draw the symbol, say an incantation like, "By the light of the moon, I cast this circle of power. May it be blessed with magic and strength."

Creating and using lunar symbols in your witchcraft is a beautiful way to deepen your connection to the moon. These symbols serve as visual reminders of the moon's presence and power, helping you align your magic with its energy. Whether you're crafting a Moon talisman, drawing symbols on your candles, or placing a lunar charm on your altar, you're inviting the moon's magic into your practice. The Moon has many faces and phases, each with its own energy and wisdom. By working with lunar symbols, you're honoring that energy and allowing it to guide you on your journey as a young witch.

So, the next time you gaze up at the moon, take note of its shape and let it inspire your magic. Draw a crescent for new adventures, a circle for completeness, or a triple Moon for balance and wisdom. Carry a Moon talisman with you as a reminder that the moon's light is always there, guiding and supporting you. With lunar symbols in your magical toolkit, you'll find that the moon's energy is never far away, ready to help you navigate your path with confidence, intuition, and a touch of moonlit magic.

The Stars and Their Magic

The stars have fascinated people for centuries. They glitter in the night sky, creating patterns that inspire stories, guide travelers, and spark dreams. For witches, the stars are not just beautiful lights in the sky; they hold ancient wisdom and magical energy that you can harness in your practice. By learning about star magic, constellations, and the influence of your star sign, you can deepen your connection to the universe and use the stars' energy to guide your journey. In this chapter, you'll be introduced to the magic of the stars, explore the power of constellations, and discover how to find your star sign.

Witches have looked to the stars for guidance and magic for as long as history has been recorded. The stars are often seen as the eyes of the universe, watching over the Earth and filling it with their light and energy. In witchcraft, star magic involves working with the energy of the stars to enhance spells, rituals, and personal growth. The stars are like magical beacons that can help you navigate your path, offering wisdom and insight when you need it most.

One of the simplest ways to connect with star magic is to spend time stargazing. On a clear night, go outside or find a spot by a window where you can see the sky. Look up and let your eyes wander across the stars. Feel their ancient energy and imagine them filling you with their light. As you gaze, take a few deep breaths and open your mind to any thoughts or feelings that arise. The stars have a way of clearing away worries and inspiring new ideas, like a magical reset button for your spirit.

The energy of the stars is perfect for spells and rituals that focus on wishes, dreams, and self-discovery. When you wish upon a star, you're not just making a simple wish; you're connecting with the star's energy and sending your intention out into the universe. Star magic can also help you gain clarity when you're feeling uncertain. By connecting with the stars, you're opening yourself to their wisdom, which can guide you toward the answers you seek.

The stars are not scattered randomly across the sky. They form patterns called constellations, which have been used by many cultures throughout history to tell stories, mark the seasons, and navigate journeys. The ancient Greeks, Romans, Egyptians, and many other civilizations saw pictures in the stars and named these constellations after animals, mythological figures, and objects. In witchcraft, constellations are seen as symbols of the different energies and qualities present in the universe.

Each constellation carries its own unique magic. For example, **Orion**, one of the most well-known constellations, is often associated with strength, bravery, and adventure. Orion is the hunter in Greek mythology, and his constellation is made up of stars that form the shape of a hunter with a belt and sword. When you look up at Orion in the night sky, you can tap into his energy to boost your courage, help you face challenges, and inspire you to go after your goals.

Another powerful constellation is **Cassiopeia**, which forms the shape of a "W" or "M" in the sky. In mythology, Cassiopeia was a queen known for her beauty and pride. Her constellation is linked to self-confidence, personal power, and beauty. Working with Cassiopeia's energy can help you embrace your unique qualities and shine with confidence. If you're ever feeling uncertain or shy, gazing up at Cassiopeia can remind you of your inner strength and the power of self-love.

The **Big Dipper** and **Little Dipper** are also famous constellations that have guided people for centuries. They are part of the larger constellations Ursa Major (the Great Bear) and Ursa Minor (the Little Bear). The Big Dipper points to the North Star, Polaris, which has been used for navigation since ancient times. In witchcraft, the North Star represents guidance, direction, and the pursuit of one's true path. When you work with the energy of the Big and Little Dippers, you're connecting with the power of the universe to guide you toward your goals and dreams.

Finding and working with constellations in your magical practice is a beautiful way to connect with the stars. On a clear night, take a moment to look up at the sky and see if you can spot some of these constellations. If you're not sure where to start, try looking for the Big Dipper. It's made up of seven bright stars and is usually easy to find. Once you've spotted it, trace the line of stars that forms the "handle" and follow it to locate the North Star. Spend a few minutes connecting with the energy of the stars you see. You might say, "Stars above, guide me with your light. Help me find my path and give me strength tonight."

In addition to constellations, your **star sign**—also known as your zodiac sign—is another way to connect with star magic. Your star sign is determined by the position of the sun on the day you were born and is part of a system called astrology. There are twelve zodiac signs, each associated with a constellation and specific traits. Your star sign can give you insight into your personality, strengths, and the kind of magic that might come naturally to you.

The twelve zodiac signs are: **Aries** (March 21 - April 19), **Taurus** (April 20 - May 20), **Gemini** (May 21 - June 20), **Cancer** (June 21 - July 22), **Leo** (July 23 - August 22), **Virgo** (August 23 - September 22), **Libra** (September 23 - October 22), **Scorpio** (October 23 - November 21), **Sagittarius** (November 22 - December 21), **Capricorn** (December 22

- January 19), **Aquarius** (January 20 - February 18), and **Pisces** (February 19 - March 20).

To find your star sign, all you need to know is your birth date. For example, if you were born on May 5th, your star sign is Taurus. Each sign is connected to a constellation that was visible in the sky when the sun was passing through that part of the zodiac. Knowing your star sign can help you understand your natural traits and how they might influence your magic. For example, if you're a **Leo**, you might naturally have a strong, creative energy that you can use in your spells and rituals. If you're a **Pisces**, you may find that dream magic and working with emotions come easily to you.

Your star sign can also guide you in working with the Moon and stars. Each zodiac sign is ruled by an element—fire, earth, air, or water—and understanding this connection can help you align your magic with the natural world. Fire signs (Aries, Leo, Sagittarius) are passionate, bold, and energetic. They often excel in spells for confidence, creativity, and action. Earth signs (Taurus, Virgo, Capricorn) are grounded, practical, and nurturing, making them natural healers and great at spells for abundance and protection. Air signs (Gemini, Libra, Aquarius) are curious, intellectual, and communicative, giving them a talent for spells related to wisdom, clarity, and inspiration. Water signs (Cancer, Scorpio, Pisces) are intuitive, emotional, and deeply connected to the unseen world, making them powerful in dream magic, intuition, and healing rituals.

To incorporate your star sign into your witchcraft, you can create a **star sign altar** that reflects your zodiac energy. Start by finding a symbol or object that represents your star sign, like a small figure of the constellation or a charm with your sign's symbol. Place it on your altar along with items that match your element. If you're a fire sign, you might include candles, red stones like carnelian, and a small bowl of sand. If you're an earth sign, add crystals like jade, herbs, and stones. For air signs, feathers, incense, and yellow stones like citrine work well. Water signs can include seashells, blue stones like aquamarine, and a small dish of Moon water.

Working with the stars can bring a sense of wonder and magic into your practice. By learning about constellations, exploring your star sign, and connecting with star energy, you're opening yourself up to the universe's ancient wisdom. Remember, the stars are always shining above you, ready to guide and inspire you on your journey. The next time you look up at the night sky, take a moment to greet the stars and feel their magic fill you with light. Your path as a Witch is intertwined with the cosmos, and the stars are there to help you navigate it with confidence and sparkle.

STAR RITUALS

The stars have always inspired wonder and magic. They twinkle above us every night, whispering secrets of the universe and reminding us of our place in the cosmos. For witches, the stars hold a special power that can be used in rituals, spells, and personal growth. By incorporating star rituals into your practice, you can tap into this celestial energy and let it guide you on your magical journey. In this chapter, we'll explore how stargazing can become a magical ritual, how to make wishes upon stars, and even how to call upon star spirits for guidance and support. These rituals will help you feel more connected to the universe and the stars' ancient wisdom.

Stargazing might seem simple, but when done with intention, it becomes a powerful ritual for any young witch. Taking time to gaze up at the night sky is an ancient practice that Witches have used for centuries to connect with the universe. The stars above us hold a quiet magic that can calm your mind, spark your imagination, and help you feel in tune with the world around you. Making stargazing a regular part of your practice allows you to develop a deeper relationship with the stars and their energy.

To turn stargazing into a ritual, find a quiet spot where you can see the night sky clearly. It might be a garden, a balcony, a park, or even a spot by a window if you're indoors. Before you begin, take a moment to set your intention. What do you want to gain from this ritual? Is it relaxation, inspiration, or perhaps a feeling of connection with the universe? Hold that intention in your mind as you start.

As you look up at the sky, let your eyes wander across the stars. Notice the patterns they make, the way they sparkle, and how they seem to tell their own stories. Breathe in deeply, letting the fresh night air fill your lungs, and as you breathe out, imagine any worries or stress leaving your body. Feel the calmness of the stars wash over you. If you can spot any familiar constellations, greet them in your mind. You might say, "Hello, Orion," or "Blessings, Cassiopeia." Connecting with the stars in this way helps build your relationship with them and makes your ritual even more meaningful.

You can also add extra magic to your stargazing ritual by bringing a crystal with you. Moonstone, selenite, or amethyst work wonderfully for star magic. Hold the crystal in your hand as you gaze at the stars, letting it soak up the celestial energy. Imagine the crystal glowing with the light of the stars, filling up with their power and wisdom. Later, you can place this crystal on your altar or use it in spells to call upon the star energy you've gathered.

Stargazing can also be used for guidance. If there's something on your mind that you're uncertain about, ask the stars for insight. Silently or aloud, say, "Stars above, shine your light upon me. Show me the way, and guide my thoughts." Then, sit quietly and watch the stars. You might not get an immediate answer, but over time, thoughts, ideas, or feelings may come to you, helping you find the clarity you seek. Trust in the stars' wisdom; they have been shining for eons and have seen countless journeys like yours.

One of the most magical and well-known star rituals is wishing upon a star. When you wish upon a star, you're not just making a simple wish; you're sending your intention out into the universe with the stars' help. It's like asking the stars to take your dreams and carry them into the cosmos, where they can gather energy and begin to manifest. Wishing upon a star can be done any time you see a star shining in the sky, but it's especially powerful when you see a shooting star.

To make your star wish, find a star that catches your eye. It might be the first star you see that evening, a particularly bright one, or a star that simply feels right. Take a deep breath and clear your mind. Look at the star and silently think about your wish. Keep it simple and clear, focusing on one wish at a time. As you hold that wish in your mind, imagine the star's light growing brighter, as if it's listening to you.

When you're ready, say your wish either aloud or in your mind. You might say, "Star light, star bright, first star I see tonight, I wish I may, I wish I might, have the wish I wish tonight." Or, you can create your own words that feel more personal to you. The important part is to truly feel the wish in your heart. Visualize it coming true, and then release the thought into the universe, trusting that the star will carry your wish forward. After you make your wish, thank the star for listening and spend a few more moments soaking up the peaceful energy of the night sky.

Another way to use star wishes is by creating a "wish jar." To do this, take a small jar and fill it with tiny pieces of paper. Each time you make a wish upon a star, write it down on a piece of paper and add it to the jar. Over time, the jar becomes filled with your dreams and intentions, a collection of your star magic. Keep the jar on your altar or a special spot in your room as a reminder of the stars' magic and your power to manifest your wishes.

In addition to making wishes, you can also call upon star spirits during your rituals and spells. In witchcraft, star spirits are seen as guardians or guides that reside in the stars, watching over the world and offering their wisdom to those who seek it. By calling upon these spirits, you can ask for their guidance, support, and protection in your magical work. The idea of star spirits can vary depending on different traditions and beliefs, but for many witches, they represent the ancient, wise energy of the stars.

To call upon star spirits, begin by finding a quiet, peaceful place where you can see the stars. Close your eyes and take several deep breaths to calm your mind. When you feel ready, open your eyes and gaze up at the stars. Choose one star to focus on, one that seems to stand out or call to you. As you look at the star, imagine its light connecting with you, like a gentle beam reaching down from the sky. Feel this light surround you, filling you with a sense of calm and protection.

Then, speak your intention. You might say, "Star spirits, ancient and wise, I call upon your light and guidance. Protect me, guide me, and help me see clearly on my path." Speak from your heart and let your words flow naturally. There's no right or wrong way to call upon star spirits; it's about creating a connection that feels meaningful to you. After you've spoken, spend a few moments in silence, listening and feeling the stars' energy around you. You may feel a sense of warmth, calmness, or a gentle nudge of intuition. Trust whatever comes to you.

If you wish, you can offer a small token of gratitude to the star spirits. This could be a simple act like placing a crystal or flower outside under the stars, lighting a candle, or even drawing a star symbol in the dirt or sand. Offering gratitude helps strengthen your connection with the star spirits and shows respect for their guidance and support.

Calling upon star spirits can also be part of your spells. If you're casting a spell for protection, light a candle on your altar and call upon the star spirits to surround you with their light. If you're doing a spell for clarity or guidance, ask the star spirits to illuminate your path and show you the way. Incorporating star spirits into your rituals adds an extra layer of magic, helping you connect more deeply with the universe and its ancient wisdom.

Star rituals are a beautiful way to bring the magic of the cosmos into your practice. Whether you're stargazing for guidance, wishing upon a star, or calling upon star spirits, you're tapping into the stars' endless energy and wisdom. The stars have been shining for millennia, guiding travelers, inspiring stories, and lighting up the night sky with their magic. By working with the stars, you're becoming part of this timeless tradition, learning to navigate your own path with the stars as your guides.

So the next time you look up at the night sky, remember that you're not just seeing stars; you're connecting with ancient magic that has been part of the universe for as long as time itself. Let the stars fill you with their light, guide you with their energy, and help you turn your dreams into reality.

Using Stars in Spells

Stars have always been a symbol of magic and wonder. Their soft, twinkling light reminds us that there is beauty and power in the universe, even in the darkest times. As a young witch, you can use the stars' energy to enhance your spells, create protective charms, draw inspiration, and bless new beginnings. The stars are there to guide you, help you grow, and light up your path with their ancient magic. In this chapter, you'll learn how to use stars in your spells, create star charms for protection, draw energy from the stars, and give star blessings for new beginnings.

When you think of protection, stars may not be the first thing that comes to mind. However, their constant presence in the sky makes them perfect symbols of guardianship and strength. Creating a star charm for protection is a wonderful way to carry a bit of the stars' energy with you, wherever you go. This charm acts like a tiny shield, using the stars' light to protect you from negativity and bring a sense of safety into your life.

To create a star charm for protection, you'll need a small piece of jewelry, a stone shaped like a star, or even a small piece of paper on which you've drawn a star. If you have a star-shaped pendant, bracelet, or keychain, you can use that as the base for your charm. Begin by sitting quietly with your chosen object. Hold it in your hands and close your eyes, taking a few deep breaths to center yourself. Picture a bright star shining high in the sky. Imagine its light growing stronger and more radiant, filling the space around you with a warm, protective glow.

As you focus on this star, visualize a beam of its light traveling down from the sky and into the charm you're holding. Imagine the charm soaking up this starry energy, becoming filled with its protective power. While doing this, say a simple incantation like, "Star bright, star light, guard me through day and night. With this charm, I hold your power, protecting me every hour." Repeat this incantation three times, feeling the energy building with each word.

After you've finished, carry the charm with you or place it somewhere important, like under your pillow, in your bag, or on your altar. Whenever you feel the need for protection, hold your star charm and imagine its light surrounding you, forming a protective shield. Remember, this charm holds the stars' strength, and just like the stars in the sky, it will always be there to guide and protect you.

Stars are not only symbols of protection but also powerful sources of energy. Drawing energy from the stars can boost your magical work, fill you with inspiration, and help you feel more connected to the universe. One of the simplest ways to draw energy from the stars is by creating a star-gathering ritual. This ritual is perfect when you're feeling low on energy, creativity, or confidence and need a cosmic boost.

To begin, find a place where you can see the stars clearly. It might be your backyard, a balcony, or a window with a view of the night sky. Stand or sit comfortably, close your eyes, and take a few deep breaths. As you breathe, imagine your body becoming calm and open, ready to receive the stars' light. When you feel centered, open your eyes and look up at the stars. Choose one star that stands out to you, one that seems to shine a little brighter or feels like it's calling to you.

Gaze at this star and imagine its light growing stronger. Picture its energy flowing down through the sky, like a stream of sparkling light that gently wraps around you. Feel this star's energy filling you up, bringing warmth, calmness, and strength. You might say an affirmation, such as, "Stars above, shine down on me. Fill me with your light and energy." As you say these words, visualize the star's light entering your body, traveling to every part of you, and filling you with a sense of power and peace.

Stay in this space for as long as you like, drawing in the star's energy. When you're ready, take a deep breath and imagine the light settling inside you, becoming part of your own energy. Thank the star for its gift and close the ritual by saying, "I carry your light within me." This ritual is a beautiful way to connect with the stars whenever you need an extra boost of cosmic energy. You can even combine this ritual with meditation, spell work, or journaling to enhance your magic.

The stars also hold the power to bless new beginnings, making them ideal to call upon when you're starting something new in your life. Whether it's a new project, a friendship, a change in your routine, or a fresh goal, a star blessing can fill that new beginning with hope, positivity, and guidance. The stars' energy encourages growth and change, just as they've guided explorers and dreamers throughout history.

To perform a star blessing for a new beginning, you'll need a small object that represents what you're starting. It could be a notebook for a new hobby, a photo of a place you want to visit, or even a piece of jewelry that you can wear to remind you of your new journey. Go outside or sit by a window where you can see the stars. Hold the object in your hands, close your eyes, and take a few deep breaths to focus your mind on your new beginning. Think about what this change means to you, what you hope to achieve, and how you want to grow.

Open your eyes and look up at the stars. Choose one that feels right to you, one that seems to shine with a special kind of light. As you gaze at this star, imagine its light shining down on you and the object you're holding. Feel the light filling the object with warmth, hope, and positivity. Say, "Stars above, bright and wise, bless this path with open skies. Guide my steps, light my way, bless this journey, night and day."

Imagine the star's light forming a protective glow around the object, blessing it with the stars' ancient wisdom and magic. Hold this image in your mind for a moment, then gently breathe out, sealing the blessing into the object. Keep this object close to you as you begin your new journey, letting it remind you of the stars' guidance and support.

Star blessings are also wonderful to use in spells for setting intentions. For example, if you're starting a new habit, like journaling or meditation, you can bless your journal or meditation space with star energy to help you stay focused and motivated. When you perform these blessings, you're not just asking the stars to guide you; you're also inviting their light to shine on your path, illuminating your way forward.

Using stars in your spells adds an extra layer of magic to your practice. Their energy is ancient, wise, and constantly present in the sky, offering guidance and protection whenever you need it. Whether you're creating a star charm for protection, drawing energy from the stars for your personal power, or performing a star blessing for a new beginning, you're aligning your magic with the cosmos and its endless possibilities.

The next time you see the stars twinkling above you, take a moment to feel their presence and remember that you're part of a vast universe filled with magic and light. The stars are always there, watching over you, ready to offer their energy, wisdom, and guidance. As you continue your journey as a young witch, let the stars be your companions, lighting up your path and helping you harness your inner power. With their magic by your side, there's no limit to the spells you can cast, the dreams you can pursue, and the light you can shine into the world. So go ahead, make your star charms, draw in their energy, and bless your new beginnings, knowing that the stars' magic is always with you.

Astrology and the Moon

The Moon has always been a magical presence in our lives, lighting up the night sky and affecting the tides, plants, and even our emotions. In astrology, the Moon represents your inner self—the part of you that feels, dreams, and reacts to the world around you. While most people know their sun sign (which is based on the day they were born), not everyone knows about their Moon sign. Your Moon sign gives you insight into your emotional world, your deepest needs, and how you handle your feelings. Understanding your Moon sign can help you navigate your magical journey with more self-awareness and guide you in harnessing your powers in a way that feels natural to you.

A Moon sign is like the secret part of your astrological identity. It's determined by the position of the Moon in the zodiac at the exact moment you were born. While your sun sign describes your outer personality and how you present yourself to the world, your Moon sign reflects who you are on the inside—your emotional core, instincts, and what makes you feel safe and secure. For witches, understanding your Moon sign is especially important because it connects you with the moon's energy, helping you align your magic with your inner self.

Each Moon sign carries different traits and qualities based on the zodiac sign the Moon was in when you were born. For example, if you have a Moon sign in Cancer, you might be naturally nurturing, sensitive, and deeply connected to your emotions. If your Moon sign is in Aries, you might feel your emotions in a fiery and direct way, often reacting quickly and passionately. Knowing your Moon sign helps you understand how you process emotions, what you need to feel comfortable and supported, and how you can use these qualities in your magical practice.

Finding your Moon sign is a fun and enlightening process. To discover it, you need to know your exact birth date, time, and place. The Moon moves quickly through the zodiac, changing signs about every two and a half days. This means that even people born just hours apart can have different Moon signs! Once you have your birth information, you can use a Moon sign calculator online or consult an astrology chart to find out which sign the Moon was in when you were born.

There are plenty of free Moon sign calculators available online. Simply enter your birth date, time, and location, and the calculator will reveal your Moon sign. You can also look up a birth chart, which maps out the positions of all the planets (including the moon) at the time of your birth. Your Moon sign will be listed among the other signs on the chart. If you don't know your exact birth time, don't worry! You can still make a pretty good guess about your Moon sign, especially if you know the general time of day you were born.

Once you've found your Moon sign, it's time to explore what it means and how it influences your emotions and magic. Each of the twelve Moon signs has its own unique set of traits that describe how you feel, react, and connect with others. Let's take a look at the characteristics of each Moon sign to help you understand your own Moon sign better.

Aries Moon: If you have an Aries moon, you experience emotions in a direct, passionate, and fiery way. You're likely to feel things intensely and take action based on your feelings. When something excites you, you throw yourself into it wholeheartedly, but you can also be quick to anger if things don't go as planned. In your magical practice, you might be drawn to spells that involve action, courage, and self-expression. To harness your Aries Moon energy, try using fire-related tools, like candles or red crystals, in your spells.

Taurus Moon: A Taurus Moon means you have a deep need for security, comfort, and stability. You're naturally grounded, patient, and enjoy the simple pleasures in life, like a cozy blanket or a delicious treat. Your emotions are steady, and you don't easily get swept away by drama. In magic, you may be drawn to earth-based practices, like working with plants, crystals, or creating charms for prosperity and protection. To nurture your Taurus moon, incorporate elements like soil, plants, and soothing scents into your rituals.

Gemini Moon: If your Moon sign is Gemini, your emotions are influenced by your mind. You're naturally curious, social, and love to talk about your feelings and thoughts. You might find that your moods can change quickly, depending on what's happening around you. In your magical practice, you may be drawn to spells that involve communication, learning, and creativity. To connect with your Gemini Moon energy, try journaling, creating sigils with words, or using air-related tools like feathers in your spells.

Cancer Moon: A Cancer Moon gives you a deep connection to your emotions and intuition. You're naturally nurturing, sensitive, and often feel a strong need to care for others. Your moods can ebb and flow like the tides, and you might find that spending time near water or in peaceful places helps you feel centered. In magic, you might be drawn to spells that involve healing, protection, and self-care. To harness your Cancer Moon energy, use water in your rituals, like Moon water or sea shells, and create cozy, nurturing spaces for your practice.

Leo Moon: With a Leo moon, you have a warm, generous, and passionate emotional nature. You feel things deeply and love to express your emotions in bold, creative ways. When you're happy, it's like the sun shines brighter, but when you're upset, it can feel like a dramatic storm. In your magical practice, you may be drawn to spells that involve self-confidence, creativity, and personal power. To connect with your Leo moon, use fire-related tools, like candles, sun symbols, or golden crystals, in your rituals.

Virgo Moon: A Virgo Moon means you're practical, thoughtful, and have a strong need for order and routine in your emotional life. You're often very tuned into the details of how you feel, and you might find comfort in organizing your thoughts or surroundings. In magic, you may be drawn to spells that involve healing, organization, and self-improvement. To nurture your Virgo moon, incorporate earth elements like herbs, plants, and green crystals into your spells and create routines that support your well-being.

Libra Moon: If you have a Libra moon, you're naturally inclined toward harmony, balance, and beauty. Your emotions are deeply connected to your relationships, and you often seek peace and fairness in your interactions. In your magical practice, you may be drawn to spells that focus on love, friendship, and balance. To connect with your Libra Moon energy, use symbols of balance, like scales, or work with crystals that promote harmony, such as rose quartz.

Scorpio Moon: A Scorpio Moon means you experience emotions with intensity and depth. You're naturally intuitive, mysterious, and have a strong need for privacy in your emotional life. When you feel something, you feel it powerfully, and you're not afraid to explore the deeper, sometimes darker, aspects of your emotions. In magic, you might be drawn to spells that involve transformation, protection, and uncovering hidden truths. To harness your Scorpio Moon energy, use water-related tools like Moon water or black crystals like obsidian in your rituals.

Sagittarius Moon: If your Moon sign is Sagittarius, you have a free-spirited, adventurous approach to emotions. You need a sense of freedom and are always seeking knowledge, wisdom, and new experiences. You're optimistic and enjoy exploring different perspectives. In your magical practice, you may be drawn to spells that involve travel, learning, and expanding your horizons. To connect with your Sagittarius moon, use fire-related tools like candles, incense, or symbols of arrows in your rituals.

Capricorn Moon: A Capricorn Moon gives you a practical, responsible, and sometimes reserved emotional nature. You're focused on achieving your goals and often prefer to keep your feelings in check, showing your emotions in a calm, steady way. In magic, you might be drawn to spells that involve protection, ambition, and building long-term success. To nurture your Capricorn Moon energy, use earth elements like stones, crystals, and symbols of mountains in your spells.

Aquarius Moon: With an Aquarius moon, you have an independent, unique, and often intellectual emotional nature. You value freedom, individuality, and being true to yourself. Your feelings are often influenced by your thoughts, and you enjoy exploring new ideas and possibilities. In your magical practice, you may be drawn to spells that involve innovation, communication, and social change. To connect with your Aquarius moon, use air-related tools like feathers, incense, or symbols of stars in your rituals.

Pisces Moon: A Pisces Moon means you're deeply sensitive, intuitive, and connected to the unseen world. Your emotions are like a vast ocean, filled with dreams, imagination, and compassion. You often feel the emotions of others, making you a natural empath. In magic, you might be drawn to spells that involve healing, dream work, and spiritual connection. To nurture your Pisces Moon energy, use water in your rituals, like Moon water or shells, and work with calming crystals like amethyst.

Understanding your Moon sign is a powerful tool in your magical practice. It not only helps you understand your emotional world better but also guides you in choosing the types of spells and rituals that resonate with your natural energy. By aligning your magic with your Moon sign, you're working with your true self, allowing your spells to flow more naturally and effectively. So embrace your Moon sign and let it be your guide as you navigate your journey as a young witch, always connected to the moon's light and your inner magic.

Moon Signs in Witchcraft

Your Moon sign is like the key to your emotional world, revealing how you feel, react, and what you need to feel secure and happy. It represents your inner self, the part of you that connects deeply with magic, dreams, and intuition. For a young witch, understanding your Moon sign can make your spells and rituals even more powerful because it allows you to work with your natural energy. In this chapter, we'll explore how to use your Moon sign in spells, create Moon sign rituals for self-discovery, and align your magic with the unique qualities of your Moon sign.

One of the best ways to use your Moon sign in witchcraft is to incorporate its traits into your spells. Each Moon sign has specific strengths, emotions, and ways of interacting with the world. When you know your Moon sign, you can tailor your spells to match your natural energy, making them more effective. For example, if your Moon sign is in fiery Aries, you might find that your magic works best when it's direct, passionate, and action-oriented. You could create spells that focus on courage, confidence, and getting things done quickly.

To use your Moon sign in your spells, start by thinking about the qualities associated with your sign. If your Moon sign is Taurus, for instance, you likely have a steady, patient nature and a deep connection to the earth. Spells that involve grounding, protection, and abundance are a great match for your energy. Try a spell that uses earth elements like crystals, plants, or soil. For example, you might create a "Prosperity Jar" filled with green crystals, herbs like basil or mint, and a small coin to attract abundance into your life. As you build the jar, focus on your intention and feel your Moon sign's grounded energy flowing into the spell.

If your Moon sign is in a water sign, like Cancer, Scorpio, or Pisces, your spells might be more effective when they involve emotions, intuition, and the element of water. A Moon water ritual, where you charge water under the moonlight and use it in your magic, can be particularly powerful. You can create a self-love spell by using Moon water in a bath ritual, adding rose petals and a few drops of lavender oil. While you soak, imagine the water washing away negative thoughts and filling you with compassion and self-care.

Air Moon signs like Gemini, Libra, and Aquarius are naturally inclined toward communication, ideas, and mental clarity. For these signs, spells that involve writing, speaking, or using symbols can be very effective. If you have an air Moon sign, try creating a "Wish Wind Spell." Write down your wish on a small piece of paper, fold it, and place it in a small pouch. On a windy night, go outside, hold the pouch up to the wind, and say, "Air and stars, carry my wish afar. Bring it to me, bright as you are." Let the wind take your wish, trusting that it will return to you in its own time.

For earth Moon signs like Taurus, Virgo, and Capricorn, working with physical objects, nature, and routines can make your spells more powerful. You might create a crystal grid for healing, using stones that align with your Moon sign's traits. Arrange the crystals in a pattern on your altar or a flat surface, placing a central stone that represents your intention. As you place each crystal, focus on its energy and how it contributes to your spell. Your earth Moon sign's natural patience and practicality will help you build a stable foundation for your magic.

Rituals are an important part of witchcraft because they create space for self-reflection, growth, and magical practice. When you align your rituals with your Moon sign, you're tuning into your inner world and discovering more about what makes you unique. Creating Moon sign rituals for self-discovery can help you explore your feelings, understand your needs, and strengthen your magical skills.

One simple yet powerful ritual is to create a "Moon Sign Altar." Choose a spot in your room where you can set up a small altar dedicated to your Moon sign. Gather items that represent the qualities of your Moon sign and place them on your altar. For example, if your Moon sign is Leo, you might include a candle, sun symbols, or golden crystals like citrine or amber. If your Moon sign is Cancer, you could add a shell, a bowl of water, and a moonstone.

Once your altar is set up, spend a few minutes each day or week sitting quietly in front of it. Light a candle and focus on the items you've placed there. Close your eyes and take a few deep breaths, imagining the energy of your Moon sign filling you up. Think about how your Moon sign influences your feelings and actions. You can ask yourself questions like, "What do I need to feel safe?" or "How can I express my emotions in a healthy way?" Let your intuition guide you, and trust any thoughts, feelings, or images that come to mind.

Another ritual for self-discovery is a "Moon Sign Meditation." Find a quiet, comfortable space and sit or lie down. Close your eyes and take several deep breaths to relax. Visualize the Moon in the sky, shining down on you with a soft, glowing light. As you breathe, imagine this light filling you, connecting you to your Moon sign's energy. Focus on how this energy feels. Is it warm and fiery, like an Aries moon, or calm and gentle, like a Pisces moon? Allow yourself to experience the sensations, thoughts, or emotions that arise. This meditation helps you connect with your inner self and gain insights into how your Moon sign shapes your feelings and reactions.

You can also use Moon sign rituals for guidance when you're facing a decision or need support. If you're feeling uncertain or overwhelmed, sit in front of your Moon sign altar, hold a crystal that resonates with your Moon sign, and ask for guidance. Say, "Moon of my sign, guide my heart. Show me the path where I should start." Then, sit quietly and listen to your intuition. Your Moon sign's energy will help you find the clarity and strength you need.

Aligning your magic with your Moon sign is all about working with your natural rhythm and energy. When you create spells and rituals that match your Moon sign, you're tapping into the deepest parts of yourself, allowing your magic to flow more freely and powerfully. Here are some ways to align your magic with your Moon sign to enhance your practice:

First, pay attention to the moon's phases. Your Moon sign may feel especially strong during certain phases of the moon. For example, if your Moon sign is in a water sign like Cancer, Scorpio, or Pisces, you might feel more connected during the full Moon when emotions are at their peak. Use this time for spells that focus on intuition, healing, or releasing what no longer serves you. If your Moon sign is in an earth sign like Taurus, Virgo, or Capricorn, you might feel more grounded and focused during the new moon, making it an ideal time to set intentions and plan for future goals.

You can also align your daily routines with your Moon sign's traits. If your Moon sign is in a fire sign like Aries, Leo, or Sagittarius, you might benefit from starting your day with an energizing ritual, like lighting a candle and setting an intention for the day. This helps you tap into your natural enthusiasm and drive. If your Moon sign is in an air sign like Gemini, Libra, or Aquarius, try incorporating journaling into your nightly routine. Write down your thoughts, feelings, and any dreams or ideas that came to you during the day. This allows you to process your emotions in a way that aligns with your air moon's need for clarity and communication.

In your spells, use symbols, colors, and elements that resonate with your Moon sign. If your Moon sign is Capricorn, try working with dark stones like obsidian or onyx for protection spells. If your Moon sign is Libra, incorporate rose quartz or symbols of balance into your love and harmony spells. These small details help you connect with your Moon sign's energy, making your magic more personal and effective.

Lastly, don't be afraid to explore and experiment with different forms of magic that align with your Moon sign. If your Moon sign is in a creative sign like Leo or Pisces, try incorporating art, music, or dance into your rituals. If your Moon sign is in a practical sign like Taurus or Virgo, you might enjoy spellcraft that involves crafting charms, growing herbs, or creating magical tools. Your Moon sign is a guide that shows you how to use your unique qualities to enhance your magic.

Understanding and working with your Moon sign is a powerful way to deepen your connection to witchcraft. It helps you align your spells and rituals with your natural strengths, emotions, and instincts, making your magic more authentic and effective. By using your Moon sign in spells, creating rituals for self-discovery, and aligning your practices with its energy, you're embracing your inner self and letting your true magic shine. So, the next time you cast a spell or perform a ritual, remember to call upon the power of your Moon sign. It's your magical ally, always there to guide you through the rhythms of the Moon and the magic within you.

Understanding Lunar Transits

The Moon is constantly on the move. As it travels through the sky, it passes through each of the twelve zodiac signs, spending about two to three days in each sign before moving on to the next. This journey is known as the moon's transit through the zodiac, and it's something every Witch should understand because it can have a powerful effect on your emotions, energy, and magical practice. The moon's transits influence how we feel and interact with the world, and by learning to work with these cycles, you can align your magic with the moon's energy for more effective spells and rituals.

The moon's path through the zodiac is like a cosmic dance. As it moves from sign to sign, it takes on the characteristics of each one, affecting the way we experience our emotions and the energy around us. For example, when the Moon is in fiery Aries, you might feel a boost in energy, courage, and a desire to take action. When it's in calm and grounded Taurus, you may feel a need to slow down, find comfort, and focus on practical matters. Understanding this constant shift in lunar energy can help you tune into your own emotions and use them to guide your magical work.

To keep track of the moon's transits, you can use a lunar calendar or a Moon app that shows you which sign the Moon is in each day. By paying attention to the moon's position in the zodiac, you can align your spells and rituals with the energy it brings. Each Moon transit offers unique opportunities for magic, so knowing the moon's current sign can give you clues about what kind of magic will work best at any given time.

For example, when the Moon is in Gemini, it's a great time to focus on spells for communication, learning, and creativity. You might feel more social, curious, and eager to explore new ideas. This transit's airy, lively energy is perfect for casting spells that involve writing, speaking, or connecting with others. You could use this time to write affirmations, create sigils, or perform a spell to enhance your study habits.

When the Moon moves into Cancer, emotions may run deeper, and you might feel more sensitive and in touch with your intuition. This is an ideal time for spells related to home, family, and self-care. If you've been feeling the need to cleanse your space or create a protective charm for your home, Cancer's nurturing energy can support those intentions. You might light a candle, take a bath with Moon water, or create a cozy space to meditate and listen to your inner feelings.

As the Moon continues its journey through each sign, it brings different influences that you can tap into for your magic. When it's in fiery Leo, the energy is bold, confident, and creative, making it a perfect time for spells that focus on self-expression, courage, and manifesting your goals. Use this transit to do a ritual that celebrates your achievements, boosts your confidence, or attracts positive attention to a project or dream you're working on.

When the Moon is in Virgo, you might feel more organized, focused, and inclined to take care of the details in your life. This is a great time to work on spells that involve healing, self-improvement, and creating order. Use Virgo's practical energy to cleanse your magical tools, organize your altar, or create a plan for your magical studies. You could also brew an herbal tea for health or set intentions for daily habits that support your well-being.

As the Moon passes through each sign, it affects not only how you feel but also how your magic flows. By understanding these lunar transits, you can choose the right time for different kinds of spells, increasing the chances that your magic will be successful. For example, if you're planning to do a spell for new beginnings, wait for the Moon to be in a fire sign like Aries or Leo for a burst of motivation and courage. If you're doing a spell for abundance, the Moon in Taurus or Capricorn provides the earthy, grounding energy needed to attract lasting prosperity.

You might wonder, how do these lunar transits specifically affect your magic? The answer lies in the moon's connection to your emotions and inner world. The Moon is like a mirror, reflecting different energies back to us as it moves through the zodiac. When you align your magic with these changing energies, you're working in harmony with the universe, which can make your spells feel more natural and powerful.

During certain transits, you may notice that some types of magic feel easier to perform than others. For example, when the Moon is in Libra, a sign of balance and harmony, spells related to love, relationships, and peace tend to flow smoothly. The energy of Libra encourages cooperation, beauty, and fairness, so it's a wonderful time to perform spells that seek to mend friendships, attract love, or create balance in your life.

On the other hand, when the Moon is in Scorpio, you might feel drawn to explore deeper, more intense forms of magic. Scorpio's energy is mysterious, transformative, and sometimes a little dark. It's perfect for shadow work, protection spells, and anything that involves looking inward to confront your fears or hidden desires. You can use this time to create a spell jar for emotional protection or a charm to help you face challenges with strength and resilience.

Paying attention to how you feel during different Moon transits can also help you understand your natural rhythms and what kind of magic works best for you. You might find that when the Moon is in certain signs, like your own Moon sign, you feel more aligned and confident in your magical work. When the Moon is in other signs, you might feel more introspective or energized. Noticing these patterns can guide you in choosing the best times for spells, rituals, and self-care.

Working with the moon's transit cycles is like riding the waves of the universe. Instead of fighting against the natural flow of energy, you're using it to your advantage. Here are some tips on how to incorporate lunar transits into your magical practice:

1. **Create a Lunar Magic Journal:** Keep a journal to track the moon's transits and how they affect you. Each day, write down which sign the Moon is in, how you're feeling, and any spells or rituals you perform. Over time, you'll start to notice patterns. You might discover that you feel particularly energized when the Moon is in Sagittarius or more reflective when it's in Pisces. These insights can help you plan your magical work around the moon's cycle.

2. **Plan Your Spells with the Moon:** Use a lunar calendar to plan your spells according to the moon's transits. If you want to work on a self-love spell, look for a day when the Moon is in Leo or Libra. For

spells related to communication or learning, wait for the Moon in Gemini. By aligning your spells with the moon's energy, you give them an extra boost and make them more likely to succeed.

3. **Perform a Lunar Transit Ritual:** When the Moon enters a new sign, take a few moments to connect with its energy. Sit quietly and close your eyes. Visualize the Moon moving through the sky and imagine it glowing with the colors and qualities of its current sign. For example, if the Moon is in Capricorn, imagine it surrounded by earthy, grounding energy. Say a simple affirmation like, "I welcome the moon's energy in [current sign] to guide my magic and my heart." This ritual helps you tune into the moon's energy and sets the tone for your magical work during the transit.

4. **Work with Your Own Moon Sign:** When the Moon transits into your Moon sign (the sign the Moon was in when you were born), it's an especially powerful time for self-discovery and magic. Use this time to perform a spell that aligns with your Moon sign's traits. If your Moon sign is Scorpio, try a ritual that involves deep emotional healing or transformation. If it's Virgo, focus on spells for health, organization, or self-care. This is a great time to nurture yourself and strengthen your connection to your Moon sign's energy.

5. **Create Moon Transit Talismans:** You can also create small talismans to carry the energy of specific lunar transits. For example, if you're working on a long-term goal, make a talisman when the Moon is in Capricorn. Hold a small stone or piece of jewelry in your hand during this transit and imagine it absorbing Capricorn's determined, patient energy. Whenever you need a boost of that energy, hold the talisman and remember the moon's influence.

Understanding lunar transits and working with the moon's cycles is a key part of navigating your powers as a witch. It helps you connect with the changing energies around you, making your magic feel more natural and in sync with the universe. By aligning your spells, rituals, and self-care practices with the moon's path through the zodiac, you're riding the cosmic waves rather than swimming against them. This harmony with the moon's energy not only makes your magic stronger but also helps you understand yourself on a deeper level.

So, the next time you're planning a spell or feeling uncertain about how to use your magic, look to the moon's transit for guidance. The Moon is always there, moving through the sky, changing and reflecting the energies of the zodiac. By tuning into its journey, you're learning to navigate your own path as a young witch, using the moon's light to guide you through every phase and cycle of life. With the moon's energy by your side, there's no limit to

the magic you can create and the dreams you can turn
into reality.

Eclipses and Their Power

The Moon has a way of lighting up the night sky, watching over the world with its calming glow. But every so often, something magical and mysterious happens—the moon's light suddenly darkens, and the sky takes on a whole new energy. This is known as a lunar eclipse, a rare and powerful event that Witches have been fascinated by for centuries. Eclipses are special times when the moon's magic becomes even more intense, offering an opportunity for transformation, reflection, and powerful spells. In this chapter, you'll learn all about lunar eclipses, the myths and magic surrounding them, and how to harness their energy through rituals.

A lunar eclipse occurs when the Earth passes directly between the sun and the moon, blocking the sunlight that usually reflects off the moon's surface. During a lunar eclipse, the Moon can appear to turn a deep red or orange color, creating a dramatic sight that has captivated people throughout history. This color change is why lunar eclipses are often called "blood moons." The eclipse typically lasts for a few hours, but its energy can be felt for days before and after the event.

Lunar eclipses only happen during a full moon, which means their energy is linked to the moon's cycle of culmination and release. When a lunar eclipse occurs, it's like a full moon's energy turned up to the max. It brings an intense focus on emotions, inner truths, and changes that need to happen in your life. This is a time when things that have been hidden or ignored may come to the surface, asking you to take a closer look and make necessary changes.

For witches, a lunar eclipse is a powerful time for deep transformation. It's like the universe pressing the pause button, giving you a chance to step back, reflect, and reset your intentions. The moon's light being covered by the Earth's shadow symbolizes a journey inward, where you can explore your emotions, uncover hidden desires, and let go of anything that no longer serves you. It's the perfect time to work on spells for release, shadow work (exploring the parts of yourself that you usually keep hidden), and powerful shifts in your energy.

Throughout history, lunar eclipses have been surrounded by myths and magical beliefs. In ancient times, people often saw eclipses as signs from the gods or messages from the universe. Some cultures believed that a lunar eclipse was a time when the Moon was battling against dark forces, while others saw it as a moment of great change, a time when the veil between the worlds was thin, allowing for a deeper connection to magic.

In some traditions, lunar eclipses were seen as times of caution and respect. People would stay indoors, quiet and reflective, to honor the moon's journey through the shadow. For witches, this idea of stepping back and reflecting during an eclipse is still important today. It's a reminder that not all magic is about action; sometimes, the most powerful spells come from sitting with your emotions, listening to your intuition, and allowing yourself to change.

The magic of a lunar eclipse is unique because it combines the energies of the full Moon and the shadow. During a regular full moon, the energy is outward and expansive, perfect for manifesting dreams and celebrating successes. But during an eclipse, the energy turns inward, inviting you to explore your inner world and release anything holding you back. This is why many Witches use lunar eclipses for shadow work, emotional healing, and letting go of old patterns that are no longer needed.

If you're new to working with lunar eclipses, it's helpful to approach them with an open heart and a sense of curiosity. Eclipses can feel intense, but they're also opportunities for growth and transformation. The key is to listen to what the Moon is showing you during this time and to use its energy to support your own journey of self-discovery.

There are many ways to work with the energy of a lunar eclipse, but one of the most powerful is through ritual. A ritual for a lunar eclipse doesn't have to be complicated; the most important thing is that it feels meaningful to you and aligns with what you want to release or transform in your life. Here are some ideas to help you create your own lunar eclipse ritual.

To begin, set up a sacred space where you can sit quietly and connect with the moon's energy. If possible, find a spot where you can see the eclipse or at least be in a place that feels calm and safe. Light a candle, place crystals like moonstone or black obsidian around you, and gather any tools you might want to use, like a journal, a small bowl of water, or a piece of paper and pen.

Start your ritual by taking a few deep breaths and closing your eyes. Visualize the Moon in the sky, shining brightly before the eclipse begins. As you breathe in, imagine the moon's light filling you up, and as you breathe out, release any tension or worries. Feel the energy of the eclipse building around you, creating a space where transformation is possible.

When you're ready, open your eyes and begin to reflect on what you want to release or change in your life. This could be a habit, a thought pattern, an emotion, or even a situation that has been weighing on you. Write it down on a piece of paper, being as honest and clear as you can. As you write, let your emotions flow. The lunar eclipse is a time of truth and honesty, so allow yourself to express whatever comes up.

Next, fold the paper and hold it in your hands. Close your eyes again and visualize the Moon slowly being covered by the Earth's shadow. As the light fades, imagine that the shadow is surrounding the paper in your hands, taking in all the energy of what you've written. Feel the moon's power helping you to release this energy, making space for new growth and change.

When you feel ready, open your eyes and decide how you want to release the paper. You might tear it up, burn it (safely, of course!), or place it in a bowl of water to dissolve. As you do this, say a simple incantation like, "By the moon's shadow, I release this from my heart. I let it go, and a new journey starts." Visualize the energy of what you're releasing flowing away from you, leaving you feeling lighter and clearer.

After your ritual, spend a few moments in quiet reflection. The energy of a lunar eclipse can be intense, so it's important to ground yourself. Place your hands on the ground, floor, or a piece of earth like a plant pot, and imagine the Earth's steady, calming energy flowing into you. Thank the Moon for its guidance and power, and blow out your candle to close the ritual.

Another way to work with lunar eclipse energy is through **shadow work**. This involves exploring the parts of yourself that you might usually hide or ignore, such as fears, insecurities, or past experiences that still affect you. The lunar eclipse's energy of shadow and light makes it an ideal time for this kind of inner exploration.

To do shadow work during an eclipse, find a quiet place where you can sit with your thoughts. Light a candle and take a few deep breaths. Ask yourself questions like, "What am I afraid of?" or "What old patterns am I ready to let go of?" Write down whatever comes to mind, without judgment. This is a time to be honest and compassionate with yourself. Remember, the Moon is guiding you through this process, helping you shine light on the shadowy parts of your inner world.

After you've explored your thoughts and feelings, think about how you can transform them. What would it look like to release these shadows and step into a new way of being? You might create a small charm or talisman to represent this transformation, carrying it with you as a reminder of the changes you're embracing.

Lunar eclipses are magical moments in the moon's cycle that offer powerful opportunities for growth, change, and self-discovery. They invite you to dive deep into your inner world, confront the shadows, and come out the other side transformed. While the energy of an eclipse can feel intense, it's also a gift from the universe, a chance to reset and align with your true self.

As you continue your journey as a young witch, remember that the moon's light and shadow are always there to guide you. Each lunar eclipse is a reminder that change is a natural part of life, and with every shadow comes the promise of new light. Embrace the magic of eclipses, and let their power help you navigate your path with courage, wisdom, and a heart open to transformation.

Solar Eclipses and Their Magic

While the Moon is often the focus of a witch's practice, the sun has its own magical energy that's just as powerful and influential. One of the most magical events involving the sun is a solar eclipse. During this rare and awe-inspiring moment, the Moon moves directly between the Earth and the sun, temporarily blocking the sun's light. For a short time, day turns to night, and everything seems to pause. Solar eclipses have been sources of wonder and mystery for centuries, and they hold incredible power for Witches who know how to harness their energy. In this chapter, we'll explore the magic of solar eclipses, the best spells to perform during an eclipse, and how to create a solar eclipse ritual to channel its transformative power.

A solar eclipse occurs when the Moon passes directly in front of the sun, casting a shadow on the Earth. Unlike lunar eclipses, which happen during the full moon, solar eclipses always take place during the new moon. During a total solar eclipse, the sky darkens, and the sun appears as a glowing ring around the dark silhouette of the moon. Partial solar eclipses, where only a part of the sun is covered, still create a dramatic shift in light and energy. This temporary blending of the sun and the moon's energies creates a unique, powerful atmosphere that can enhance your magical work in extraordinary ways.

In witchcraft, solar eclipses are seen as times of profound change, transformation, and new beginnings. They bring together the fiery, vibrant energy of the sun with the intuitive, mysterious energy of the moon, creating a kind of cosmic reset. The light of the sun represents our outer selves—our goals, ambitions, and the way we shine in the world. Meanwhile, the Moon represents our inner selves—our emotions, instincts, and the unseen aspects of our personality. When a solar eclipse occurs, it's like these two parts of ourselves are coming into alignment, allowing us to see things in a new light and make powerful changes.

The magic of a solar eclipse is about embracing transformation and using the energy of the moment to let go of the old and welcome the new. It's a time when the universe seems to press the "reset" button, offering a chance to release outdated habits, beliefs, or situations and set fresh intentions for the future. If you've been feeling stuck or unsure about a path forward, a solar eclipse can be a perfect opportunity to shift your energy and create a new direction for yourself.

Because solar eclipses are so rare, they're seen as moments of heightened power. In ancient cultures, eclipses were often surrounded by myths and legends, seen as moments when the veil between worlds was thin, and anything was possible. Some traditions believed that solar eclipses marked times when the sun and Moon were in deep conversation, sharing secrets and wisdom. For Witches today, solar eclipses are magical windows of time when you can harness the combined energy of the sun and Moon to amplify your spells, manifest dreams, and clear away obstacles.

When it comes to spells, solar eclipses are ideal for those that involve new beginnings, change, and transformation. The energy of a solar eclipse is all about resetting and starting fresh, making it a perfect time for spells that help you release the past and embrace a new chapter. Here are some of the best types of spells to perform during a solar eclipse:

1. **Transformation Spells**: Solar eclipses are like magical turning points. If there's something in your life that you want to change—whether it's a habit, a situation, or even a way of thinking—a solar eclipse is the perfect time to cast a spell for transformation. For this spell, light a candle and hold a small object (like a stone or charm) that represents the

change you want to make. Close your eyes and imagine the eclipse's energy filling you, surrounding you with light. Say, "By the power of the sun and moon, I embrace this change. I release the old and welcome the new." Carry the object with you as a reminder of the transformation you're working on.

2. **New Beginning Spells**: The new Moon energy of a solar eclipse is incredibly powerful for setting intentions and starting fresh. If you're beginning a new project, relationship, or phase in your life, use the eclipse to cast a spell for success and guidance. Write down your intention on a piece of paper, fold it, and hold it in your hands. As you visualize the eclipse, imagine your intention glowing with the combined light of the sun and moon. Place the paper under a small dish of water and say, "Eclipse of light and shadow, bless this new beginning. May it grow strong and true, guided by your magic." Keep the paper in a safe place, and let the water act as a symbol of nurturing your intention.

3. **Release Spells**: Solar eclipses are also excellent times for releasing what no longer serves you. The brief darkness of the eclipse represents a moment when the old can be let go, clearing the way for the new. For a release spell, write down what you want to let go of on a piece of paper. Fold the

paper and place it in a bowl of salt water. As the paper dissolves, imagine the energy of the eclipse carrying away the feelings, habits, or situations you wish to release. Say, "With the sun's shadow, I let this go. I am free, I am new." Let the water sit until the eclipse ends, then pour it into the earth to complete the spell.

A solar eclipse ritual can be a deeply transformative experience, helping you connect with the powerful energies of the sun and moon. To create your own solar eclipse ritual, start by finding a quiet place where you can sit comfortably, preferably where you can see the sky. If you're indoors, a window or a spot near natural light works well. Gather any magical tools you want to use, such as candles, crystals, a journal, or a small bowl of water.

Begin by lighting a candle to represent the sun. As you light it, close your eyes and take a few deep breaths. Imagine the warmth and light of the sun surrounding you, filling you with strength and vitality. Next, hold a moonstone or a small object that symbolizes the moon. Feel its cool, calming energy, and imagine it blending with the warmth of the sun, creating a balance within you.

As the eclipse begins (or if you're doing this ritual without watching the eclipse, simply imagine it), sit quietly and focus on the candle's flame. Visualize the Moon slowly moving in front of the sun, covering it and casting a shadow. During this time, think about what you want to release or change in your life. What old patterns are you ready to let go of? What new energy do you want to invite in?

When the eclipse reaches its peak, imagine the moment of darkness as a powerful reset. In your mind's eye, see this darkness clearing away anything that's holding you back, leaving you open and ready for new beginnings. You might say an affirmation like, "In this eclipse, I find my power. I release the past and step into the light of change."

After this, light a second candle to symbolize the return of the sun's light. As you do, visualize the darkness fading and the light returning, bringing with it the energy of renewal and transformation. Hold your moonstone or object close to your heart and say, "By the light of the sun and the guidance of the moon, I embrace my path, new and true."

End the ritual by sitting quietly for a few moments, feeling the energy of the eclipse within you. If you have a journal, write down any thoughts, feelings, or intentions that came up during the ritual. This can help you carry the energy of the eclipse forward and remind you of the changes you're embracing.

After the ritual, it's important to ground yourself, as the energy of an eclipse can be intense. Place your hands on the ground, close your eyes, and imagine roots growing from your fingers into the earth, anchoring you and bringing you back to a calm, steady state. Thank the sun and the Moon for their guidance, and blow out your candles to close the ritual.

Solar eclipses are rare and magical moments that offer a chance to embrace change, reset your energy, and set new intentions. By working with the powerful energy of these eclipses, you're tapping into the combined forces of the sun and moon, using their light and shadow to guide you through transformation. Whether you're casting spells for new beginnings, releasing old habits, or simply taking time to reflect, solar eclipses provide a unique opportunity to deepen your connection with the universe and your own inner magic.

So, the next time a solar eclipse comes around, prepare to harness its energy. Remember, the sun and Moon are always there, guiding you with their cycles. A solar eclipse is their way of reminding you that change is not only possible—it's a natural, beautiful part of life. Embrace the magic of eclipses, and let them light up your path with courage, wisdom, and endless possibilities.

ECLIPSE ENERGY ÎN WITCHCRAFT

E clipses, whether lunar or solar, are some of the most powerful cosmic events you can work with as a witch. They carry a mix of intense energies that can stir up your emotions, bring hidden truths to light, and open new paths for growth and change. The energy of an eclipse is like a bolt of magic in the air, offering a special opportunity to cleanse, manifest, and create powerful tools that you can use long after the eclipse is over. In this chapter, we'll dive into how to harness the dual energies of eclipses, use these celestial events for cleansing and manifestation, and even create your own eclipse talismans to carry their magic with you.

The magic of eclipses lies in their unique combination of energies. A solar eclipse brings together the vibrant, outward energy of the sun with the cool, introspective energy of the new moon. This combination creates a moment where light and shadow meet, allowing you to see things in a new way and make transformative changes. On the other hand, a lunar eclipse merges the emotional, intuitive energy of the full Moon with the earth's shadow, creating a powerful space for deep reflection, release, and healing.

When you harness the dual energies of an eclipse, you're working with both the light and the shadow—two sides of the same coin. This is what makes eclipse magic so special; it's about balance, transformation, and embracing all parts of yourself. During an eclipse, the universe provides a moment when the usual patterns of energy shift, opening up a window for you to work on things that might normally feel stuck or hidden.

To harness this energy, start by considering what kind of magic you want to focus on during the eclipse. A solar eclipse is perfect for spells related to new beginnings, confidence, and manifesting your dreams. It's a time when the sun's light is temporarily hidden, offering you a chance to pause, reset, and plant the seeds for your future. If you're feeling ready to start a new project, take a bold step, or set new goals, a solar eclipse is your moment to capture that energy.

A lunar eclipse, however, is best suited for magic that involves letting go, emotional healing, and inner work. During a lunar eclipse, the moon's light is overshadowed by the earth, symbolizing a journey into the depths of your emotions and subconscious. This is a powerful time to explore your feelings, release old habits, and heal past wounds. It's like the Moon is holding up a mirror, showing you what's been hidden in the shadows, so you can work on transforming it into something positive.

To tap into these dual energies, create a simple eclipse ritual that involves both reflection and intention-setting. For a solar eclipse, light a candle to represent the sun's light, then take a few moments to reflect on what you want to release and what you want to welcome into your life. Write down your intentions on a piece of paper, fold it, and place it under the candle as it burns. Imagine the eclipse's energy filling your intentions with strength and courage.

For a lunar eclipse, sit quietly with a piece of moonstone or another calming stone. Close your eyes and take deep breaths, allowing yourself to feel any emotions that come up. Imagine the moon's light turning to a soft glow, re-vealing what's been hidden within you. Write down what you're ready to let go of on a piece of paper. Tear up the paper into small pieces and scatter them in the wind or bury them in the earth, symbolizing the release of that energy. Then, light a small candle to represent the moon's return to light, visualizing a fresh start and emotional clarity.

Eclipses are also ideal for cleansing and manifesting be-cause they act as cosmic resets, clearing away old ener-gy and making room for new possibilities. You can use both lunar and solar eclipses to cleanse your magical tools, your space, or even your own energy. The temporary darkness of an eclipse represents a break in the usual flow, allowing you to sweep away negativity and welcome a clean slate.

To cleanse your tools during an eclipse, gather your crystals, wands, tarot cards, and other magical items, and place them in a circle on your altar or in a special spot where they can absorb the eclipse's energy. For a solar eclipse, do this in a sunlit area, even if it's indoors near a window. For a lunar eclipse, place your items outside or near a window where they can soak up the moon's light. As the eclipse occurs, imagine the shadow washing over your tools, clearing away any stagnant energy and recharging them with fresh power. When the eclipse ends, thank the sun or Moon for their cleansing energy, and store your tools with the intention that they are now ready for new magical work.

Manifestation during an eclipse is also a potent practice. During a solar eclipse, focus on what you want to bring into your life—whether it's new opportunities, personal growth, or specific goals. Write down your intentions and fold the paper into a small bundle. Hold it in your hands and close your eyes, visualizing the eclipse's energy filling your intentions with light and power. Keep this bundle on your altar or in a special place as a reminder of the new beginning you've set in motion.

For a lunar eclipse, focus on what you want to transform or release. This might involve emotional patterns, habits, or anything that feels heavy or restrictive. Write down what you want to release and then create a "Release Jar." Fill a small jar with salt, herbs like sage or rosemary for cleansing, and a piece of paper with what you wish to let go of. Seal the jar and place it under the moonlight during the eclipse, allowing the shadow to absorb and neutralize the energy within. After the eclipse, bury the jar or pour its contents into running water (like a river or stream) to symbolize the final release.

One of the most magical ways to work with eclipse energy is by creating an eclipse talisman. A talisman is a small object that holds specific energy or intention, and when charged during an eclipse, it becomes a powerful tool you can use in your magical practice. To create an eclipse talisman, choose an object that feels meaningful to you. This could be a crystal, a piece of jewelry, a small charm, or even a stone you find outside.

For a solar eclipse talisman, select something that reflects the sun's vibrant energy—such as a piece of sunstone, a gold-colored charm, or a bright yellow crystal like citrine. Hold the object in your hands as the eclipse begins, and close your eyes. Visualize the sun's light shining through the shadow of the moon, filling the talisman with both the strength of the sun and the mystery of the moon. Say a simple incantation like, "Sun and moon, light and shade, in this talisman, your power is made." Carry this talisman with you whenever you need a boost of courage, clarity, or inspiration.

For a lunar eclipse talisman, choose an object that represents the moon's calming, intuitive energy, such as a piece of moonstone, amethyst, or silver jewelry. As the eclipse unfolds, hold the object and imagine the moon's light merging with the earth's shadow, creating a swirl of transformative energy. Say, "Moon of shadow, Moon of light, in this talisman, guide my sight." This talisman will become a tool for emotional support, inner work, and deep reflection. Keep it on your altar or carry it with you during times of change or when you need to explore your inner world.

After creating your talisman, you can use it in spells, rituals, or meditations to call upon the eclipse's energy whenever you need it. The talisman acts as a small piece of the eclipse's magic, a reminder that you have the power to embrace change, balance light and shadow, and navigate your path with strength and wisdom.

Eclipses are extraordinary events in the Moon and sun's cycles, offering moments of powerful magic that you can harness in your witchcraft. By learning to work with the dual energies of eclipses, using them for cleansing and manifestation, and creating eclipse talismans, you're tapping into the universe's natural rhythm and using it to guide your own journey. The magic of an eclipse reminds you that light and shadow are both part of who you are, and embracing them allows you to transform, grow, and shine brightly. So, the next time an eclipse graces the sky, get ready to work with its energy and let it fill your magic with its incredible power.

CREATING A LUNAR ALTAR

C reating a lunar altar is one of the most magical and personal ways to connect with the moon's energy. An altar is like your own sacred space where you can practice spells, perform rituals, and reflect on your intentions. When you make your altar dedicated to the moon, it becomes a place filled with lunar magic, helping you feel closer to the moon's cycles and harness its power in your witchcraft. In this chapter, you'll learn how to set up your very own lunar altar, including how to choose the right space, gather the essential tools, and add personal touches that make it uniquely yours.

The first step in creating your lunar altar is choosing the perfect spot for it. This can be anywhere you feel safe, comfortable, and able to focus on your magical work. Your altar could be a small table, a windowsill, a shelf, or even a space on the floor. Some Witches like to set up their altars near a window where the moonlight can reach it, while others prefer a cozy corner in their room that feels private and peaceful. The most important thing is that it's a place where you can return to whenever you need to connect with the moon's energy.

When selecting a space, think about what kind of environment makes you feel calm and inspired. If you enjoy being surrounded by nature, you might choose a spot near plants or a window that looks out onto the garden. If you love the moon's glow, find a place where you can easily see the Moon from your altar, especially during the full Moon when its light is the brightest. You don't need a lot of room—just enough space to hold a few magical items and give you a sense of connection to the moon.

Once you've chosen your spot, it's time to cleanse the area. Cleansing is a way of clearing out any old or unwanted energy, making room for the magic you're about to create. You can cleanse your altar space using different methods, like burning sage or incense, sprinkling salt, or simply wiping it down with a cloth while focusing on your intention. As you cleanse, imagine the space filling up with fresh, clean energy, ready to hold the moon's magic. You might say, "This space is now sacred, cleansed, and pure. Ready for the moon's light, strong and sure."

After you've prepared the space, it's time to gather the essential tools for your lunar altar. These items will help you connect with the moon's energy and enhance your spells and rituals. While every witch's altar is different, here are some key tools that you might want to include on your lunar altar:

1. **Candles**: Candles are a must-have on any lunar altar. They represent the moon's light and can be used in almost every spell or ritual. White or silver candles are especially good for Moon magic, as they symbolize the moon's glow and purity. You might also include candles in colors that match the different Moon phases—like white for the full moon, black or dark blue for the new moon, and light gray or silver for the waxing and waning phases. Place one or more candles on your altar, and light them whenever you want to call upon the moon's energy.

2. **Crystals**: Crystals are natural holders of energy and make wonderful additions to a lunar altar. Moonstone is a classic choice, as it carries the calming, intuitive energy of the moon. You can also include selenite for clarity, amethyst for spiritual connection, and clear quartz to amplify the moon's power. Arrange your crystals in a way that feels right to you. Some Witches like to place them in a circle to represent the moon's cycle, while others group them based on their magical properties. Whenever you need to focus or recharge, hold one of these crystals and feel the moon's energy flowing through it.

3. **A Bowl of Water**: Since the Moon is closely con-

nected to water, having a small bowl of water on your altar is a great way to honor this element. You can use this water for Moon water rituals, or simply keep it on the altar as a symbol of the moon's influence over the tides and your emotions. If you want, add a sprinkle of salt to the water to represent the ocean, or drop in a few flower petals or herbs for an added touch of nature. Change the water regularly to keep the energy fresh and vibrant.

4. **Symbols of the Moon**: Adding symbols of the Moon to your altar helps you focus your magic and connect with lunar energy. These symbols can be anything that reminds you of the moon, such as a crescent Moon charm, a small Moon sculpture, or a drawing of the Moon phases. You might also include images of the Moon goddess, stars, or constellations. Place these symbols in the center of your altar as a focal point for your spells and rituals.

5. **Herbs and Flowers**: Some herbs and flowers are closely associated with the Moon and can enhance the energy of your altar. Lavender, jasmine, and mugwort are popular choices, as they carry calming and intuitive properties. You can keep these herbs in small bowls, jars, or sachets, or sprinkle them around your altar to create a magical atmosphere. Fresh or dried flowers, like white roses or lilies, also make beautiful additions and bring the

moon's gentle beauty into your space.

Now that you have the essential tools, it's time to add personal touches that make your altar unique. Your lunar altar should reflect who you are as a Witch and what you're currently focusing on in your magical practice. Adding personal items and decorations helps you create a space that feels special and inspiring every time you use it.

One way to personalize your altar is by including items that have personal significance. This could be a piece of jewelry that makes you feel powerful, a photo of a place where you feel connected to nature, or a small charm that you've used in past spells. These items carry your own energy and experiences, adding depth to the magic you create at your altar.

You can also decorate your altar with things that represent your Moon sign. If your Moon sign is Cancer, you might include a seashell or a small bowl of water. If it's Leo, add a golden charm or a sun symbol. These decorations help you connect with the moon's influence on your own emotional world, making your altar a place where you can explore and honor your inner self.

Another way to make your altar your own is by changing it to match the current Moon phase. For example, during the full moon, you might fill your altar with white candles, fresh flowers, and Moon symbols to celebrate the moon's bright, expansive energy. During the new moon, you could switch to darker colors, like black or deep blue, and add elements that represent new beginnings, like seeds, feathers, or an empty jar waiting to be filled. This practice helps you stay in tune with the moon's cycle and keeps your altar energy fresh and aligned with the lunar phases.

As you use your lunar altar, remember that it's a living, evolving space. Feel free to change things up, add new items, and rearrange as often as you like. Your altar grows with you and your practice, reflecting your journey as a Witch and your connection to the moon. It's a place where you can come to set intentions, cast spells, meditate, and simply be in the moon's magical presence.

Creating a lunar altar is more than just setting up a collection of objects—it's about building a sacred space where you can explore your magic and deepen your connection to the moon. By choosing a special spot, gathering the right tools, and adding personal touches, you're making a place that's uniquely yours, filled with the moon's energy and your own magical intentions. So take your time, enjoy the process, and let your altar become a magical sanctuary that you can return to whenever you need to feel the moon's power and guidance. The Moon is always there, ready to light up your path and fill your altar with its timeless magic.

Decorating with Lunar Elements

Your lunar altar is a reflection of your magical practice, a place where you can connect with the moon's energy and express your unique witchy style. Decorating your altar with lunar elements not only makes it visually beautiful but also fills it with the moon's power, helping you feel more connected to the magic you're creating. When you include elements like Moon phases, Moon crystals, symbols, and even star magic, your altar becomes a magical centerpiece that aligns with the rhythms of the cosmos. Let's dive into how you can bring these elements into your altar and make it a true lunar sanctuary.

One of the most powerful ways to decorate your altar is by incorporating the different phases of the moon. The moon's cycle has a big impact on our energy and emotions, and by adding representations of its phases to your altar, you can connect with the moon's changing energy and use it to enhance your spells and rituals.

Start by considering which Moon phase resonates with you the most or aligns with your current intentions. Each phase has its own magic. The **new Moon** is about new beginnings and setting intentions, while the **waxing Moon** (when the Moon is growing) is great for building energy, growth, and attraction spells. The **full Moon** represents abundance, clarity, and manifestation, making it the perfect time for spells to amplify your desires. Finally, the **waning Moon** (when the Moon is shrinking) is a time for release, letting go, and cleansing.

To represent these phases on your altar, you can use simple symbols and objects. For example, you can draw or print small images of the moon's phases and place them on your altar. If you want to be more creative, try painting or drawing crescent moons, full moons, and waning moons on stones or pieces of wood. You could even collect flat stones or seashells and paint them to resemble the different Moon phases, arranging them in a circle on your altar to represent the moon's cycle.

If you love working with candles, consider using candles in different colors to match the Moon phases. Use a **black or dark blue candle** for the new Moon to represent the unknown and new beginnings. For the waxing moon, light a **white or silver candle** to symbolize growing energy and attraction. On the night of the full moon, use a **bright**

white or golden candle to capture the moon's glowing energy and power. Finally, for the waning moon, a **gray or light blue candle** can represent the calming, cleansing energy of letting go.

You might also choose to change the decorations on your altar to match the current Moon phase. For example, during the new moon, you can place a small jar on your altar to symbolize the empty space ready to be filled with new intentions. During the full moon, add flowers, crystals, and other elements that represent abundance and celebration. For the waning moon, include a bowl of water or salt to represent cleansing and release. These small changes help you stay in tune with the moon's cycle and bring its energy into your magical practice.

Crystals are natural energy holders and make wonderful additions to your lunar altar. The moon's energy is calming, intuitive, and deeply connected to our emotions, and there are certain crystals that resonate strongly with this lunar magic. Moonstone is perhaps the most famous Moon crystal. It carries the gentle, soothing energy of the moon, helping you tap into your intuition and inner wisdom. Adding a piece of moonstone to your altar can enhance your spells, rituals, and meditation practices, especially those related to dreams, emotions, and self-reflection.

Another beautiful crystal to include on your lunar altar is **selenite**. Selenite has a soft, milky glow that resembles moonlight, and it's known for its cleansing and purifying properties. Keeping a selenite wand or sphere on your altar can help clear away negative energy and create a peaceful, harmonious atmosphere. You can also use selenite to cleanse other crystals on your altar by placing them next to or on top of the selenite. This way, your altar will always be charged with pure, moon-like energy.

Amethyst is another powerful moon-related crystal. Its purple color is linked to intuition, spirituality, and inner peace. Adding an amethyst crystal to your altar can deepen your connection to your intuition, making it a great tool for Moon rituals that focus on inner work, meditation, and dream magic. You can place the amethyst near the center of your altar or hold it during Moon meditations to enhance your connection to the moon's energy.

In addition to crystals, consider adding symbols that represent the moon. This could be a **crescent Moon charm**, a small Moon sculpture, or a picture of the Moon in its various phases. You can also use objects that remind you of the moon's beauty, such as **silver jewelry, pearls,** or **round stones** that resemble a full moon. If you like to craft, try making a Moon garland by cutting out shapes of the Moon phases from paper or fabric and hanging it above or around your altar. These symbols serve as focal points that help you draw in the moon's energy whenever you need it.

The Moon isn't the only celestial body that holds magic—stars are also powerful symbols of hope, guidance, and dreams. Bringing star magic into your lunar altar adds an extra layer of cosmic energy and reminds you of the vastness and beauty of the universe. Stars are like the moon's companions, lighting up the night sky and inspiring us to look beyond the ordinary.

To incorporate star magic, start by adding symbols of stars to your altar. You can use star-shaped charms, cut-out star shapes, or even draw tiny stars on pieces of paper. If you have a star-shaped crystal, like **clear quartz** or **citrine**, place it on your altar to represent the stars' bright, positive energy. You could also find a star-themed fabric or cloth to place under your altar items, creating a starry sky effect.

Another way to bring star magic into your altar is by including elements that connect you to the cosmos. For example, you might place a small jar filled with **glitter** or **sparkling sand** on your altar to represent stardust. You can use this stardust in spells to attract positivity, luck, and guidance. Sprinkle a little bit on your altar during rituals, or carry some in a small pouch to keep star energy with you throughout the day.

Consider creating a **star jar** to capture the energy of the night sky. Find a small glass jar and fill it with a mixture of **clear quartz chips, silver glitter**, and a drop of Moon water. As you fill the jar, imagine the stars' light gathering inside, filling the jar with hope, inspiration, and magic. Seal the jar and place it on your altar as a reminder that you carry the stars' light within you.

If you love constellations, use them as part of your altar decorations. Print out or draw pictures of your favorite constellations and place them around your altar. If you know your star sign, include its constellation to represent your connection to the universe. This adds a personal touch and helps you feel more aligned with the cosmic energy that influences your life and magic.

Creating and decorating your lunar altar is a magical process that allows you to express your unique connection to the Moon and stars. By incorporating Moon phases, Moon crystals, symbols, and star magic, you're filling your altar with elements that align with your practice and intentions. Each time you add a new decoration, whether it's a moonstone crystal, a crescent charm, or a jar of stardust, you're enhancing your altar's energy and making it a powerful tool for your witchcraft.

Remember, your lunar altar is your own sacred space, so decorate it in a way that feels right to you. Let your intuition guide you as you choose and arrange items, and don't be afraid to change things up to match the moon's cycles or your current focus in magic. The Moon and stars are always there, shining their light to guide you, and your altar is a place where you can connect with that energy whenever you need to. As you decorate your altar with lunar elements, you're creating a magical sanctuary where you can harness the power of the cosmos and explore your own inner magic.

Using Your Altar in Rituals

Now that your lunar altar is set up and decorated with elements that reflect the moon's energy and your own magical style, it's time to explore how to use it in your daily witchcraft rituals. Your altar is a place where you can practice magic, connect with the moon's phases, and focus your intentions. It's more than just a collection of magical tools; it's a space that holds your energy, dreams, and the magic you want to create. Whether you're blessing your altar each day, working with the moon's phases, or meditating during the full moon, your altar can help you harness the moon's power in meaningful ways. Let's dive into some rituals you can perform at your altar to deepen your practice and strengthen your connection to the moon.

A beautiful way to start each day is by performing a daily altar blessing. This simple practice helps you set the tone for the day, inviting positive energy and the moon's magic into your life. Daily blessings don't have to be complicated; they can be as quick as lighting a candle or saying a few words of intention. The key is to do something that feels right for you and aligns with the energy you want to carry throughout the day.

To begin your daily blessing, go to your altar in the morning or whenever you feel ready. Take a deep breath and focus on the items you have on your altar, whether it's candles, crystals, symbols, or Moon phases. Feel the energy in your space, and allow yourself to connect with the calm, soothing power of the moon. If you have a candle on your altar, light it and say, "By the moon's light, I bless this day. May it be filled with magic, peace, and guidance." As the flame flickers, imagine the moon's light filling your room and your heart, creating a protective and inspiring aura around you.

You might also choose to hold a crystal, such as moonstone or amethyst, while you say your blessing. Close your eyes and let the crystal's energy connect with you, filling you with its calming, intuitive power. If you like, say an affirmation like, "I welcome the moon's magic into my day. I am guided, strong, and ready to shine." Feel the warmth and comfort of the moon's energy wrapping around you, and carry that feeling with you as you go about your day.

If you want to make your daily altar blessing more interactive, you can include a simple action, such as drawing a card from an oracle or tarot deck to gain insight for the day ahead. Place the card on your altar as a reminder of the message you received, and reflect on it whenever you pass by your altar throughout the day. By starting your day with this small ritual, you're setting a magical intention and grounding yourself in the moon's energy, helping you feel more focused and connected as you move through your day.

Your lunar altar can be a powerful tool for connecting with the moon's phases. The moon's cycle has a profound effect on our emotions, energy, and intentions, so aligning your altar rituals with these phases can enhance your magic and help you feel in tune with the natural rhythms of the universe. By performing moon-phase altar rituals, you're creating a practice that evolves and flows with the changing moon, allowing you to work with its energy in different ways.

During the **new Moon,** when the sky is dark and the Moon is hidden, focus on setting intentions and planting the seeds for new beginnings. To perform a new Moon ritual at your altar, start by cleansing the space with incense or by gently waving your hands over it to clear away any lingering energy. Light a candle to represent the new moon's potential, and place a small bowl of water on the altar to symbolize the emotions and dreams you want to nurture. Write down your intentions for the upcoming lunar cycle on a piece of paper, fold it, and place it under the bowl of water. As you do this, say, "Under the new moon's shadow, I plant these seeds of light. May they grow strong and true, guided by the moon's gentle might." Leave the paper on your altar for the entire Moon cycle to remind you of your intentions.

When the Moon begins to **wax**, growing brighter each night, focus on building energy and attracting what you desire. For this phase, add elements to your altar that represent growth and positivity, such as fresh flowers, green crystals, or a jar filled with seeds or herbs. Each day, light a candle on your altar and visualize your intentions gaining strength, just as the moon's light grows in the sky. You might say an affirmation like, "As the Moon grows, so do my dreams. I attract all that I seek with grace and ease."

During the **full Moon**, when the Moon is at its brightest, your altar becomes a space of celebration, manifestation, and reflection. The full Moon is a time to acknowledge what you've accomplished and to embrace the abundance in your life. To perform a full Moon ritual at your altar, light several candles to represent the moon's radiant energy. Hold a crystal, like moonstone or selenite, in your hands, and close your eyes. Think about what you've been working towards, and take a moment to celebrate your progress. Place a bowl of water on your altar and, if possible, let the moonlight shine on it. Say, "Under the full moon's glow, I celebrate my journey. I embrace abundance and light." You can also use this water later as Moon water in other spells and rituals.

As the Moon begins to **wane**, shrinking in size each night, it's time to focus on release and cleansing. For this phase, place a small bowl of salt or sage on your altar to represent purification. Light a candle and sit quietly in front of your altar, reflecting on what you need to let go of. Write down anything you wish to release on a piece of paper, fold it, and place it in the bowl. Say, "As the Moon fades, I release what no longer serves me. I cleanse my spirit and create space for the new." Leave the paper on your altar until the next new moon, then dispose of it by burying it in the earth or casting it into water.

One of the most calming and empowering ways to use your altar is by performing a full Moon meditation. The full moon's light is powerful and illuminating, making it the perfect time to connect with your intuition and explore your inner world. Your altar, filled with lunar elements, provides the ideal setting for this practice, helping you focus your energy and deepen your meditation experience.

To begin your full Moon meditation, sit comfortably in front of your altar. Light a candle to represent the moon's glow and place a crystal, such as moonstone or amethyst, in your hand. Close your eyes and take a few deep breaths, allowing your mind and body to relax. Visualize the full Moon shining above you, casting its gentle, silvery light over your space and filling your heart with calmness.

As you breathe, imagine the moonlight growing brighter, enveloping your entire being. Feel its energy washing over you, soothing your mind, and clearing away any worries or doubts. Focus on the crystal in your hand and let its energy merge with the moon's light, amplifying your connection to your intuition. You might say silently, "Full Moon above, light my way. Show me the truths I seek today."

Spend a few minutes in this space, allowing your thoughts to drift like clouds in the moonlit sky. Notice any feelings, images, or messages that come to you. The full Moon is a time of clarity, so trust your intuition and be open to whatever insights you receive. If you like, ask the Moon for guidance on a specific question or situation. Imagine the moon's light filling your mind with wisdom, bringing the answers you seek.

When you're ready to end the meditation, take a deep breath and slowly open your eyes. Blow out the candle and place the crystal back on your altar, thanking the Moon for its guidance and energy. You might want to write down any thoughts or feelings you had during the meditation in your journal, so you can reflect on them later.

Using your lunar altar in daily blessings, moon-phase rituals, and full Moon meditations helps you build a regular practice of connecting with the moon's magic. Your altar becomes a place where you can set intentions, release what no longer serves you, and explore your inner world. It's your personal space to work with the moon's energy in a way that feels meaningful and powerful. So light your candles, hold your crystals, and let your altar guide you as you harness the magic of the Moon in your life.

LUNAR DREAMS AND MAGIC

The Moon has long been associated with dreams, magic, and the mysterious world of sleep. When the Moon rises and the world quiets down, it's as if the veil between reality and the dream world becomes thinner, allowing us to tap into a different kind of magic. As a new witch, understanding the moon's influence on dreams can help you explore the hidden corners of your mind, gain insight into your subconscious, and even strengthen your magical abilities. In this chapter, you'll learn how the Moon affects your dreams, what common dream symbols might mean, and how to remember your dreams so you can use them in your magical practice.

Have you ever noticed that your dreams feel different depending on the moon's phase? Maybe they're more vivid during the full moon, or more reflective and introspective when the Moon is new. This is because the moon's energy has a direct influence on our emotions and subconscious, making it a powerful force in the realm of dreams. Just as the Moon affects the tides, it also affects the ebb and flow of our inner world, particularly when we sleep.

The full Moon is known for intensifying emotions and bringing clarity. During this time, your dreams might be more vivid, intense, and filled with strong imagery. You may even experience what are known as "lucid dreams," where you're aware that you're dreaming and can sometimes control the dream's direction. These full Moon dreams can reveal truths about your deepest desires, fears, or thoughts that have been hiding in your subconscious. If you find that your dreams during the full Moon are more colorful and intense, this is the moon's way of showing you aspects of yourself that are ready to be explored.

On the other hand, the new Moon is a time of darkness and introspection, making it perfect for dreams that delve into your inner world. New Moon dreams can be quieter, filled with symbols of beginnings, possibilities, and reflections on what you need to release or change. These dreams often guide you toward setting new intentions, helping you see what areas of your life need a fresh start. If your dreams during the new Moon seem more mysterious or emotional, they're likely nudging you to look within and pay attention to your feelings.

The waxing and waning phases of the Moon also influence dreams in unique ways. As the Moon **waxes** and grows in light, your dreams might reflect themes of growth, attraction, and building energy. This is a good time to dream about goals, ambitions, and what you want to bring into your life. During the **waning Moon,** when the Moon is shrinking in the sky, your dreams might focus on letting go, clearing out old habits, or preparing for a time of rest. The energy of the waning Moon encourages you to release what no longer serves you, and your dreams can help guide you in understanding what that might be.

As you pay attention to the moon's phases, notice how your dreams change. Keeping a dream journal by your bed is a great way to track these changes and see how the moon's energy affects your inner world. Before going to sleep, you can set an intention to connect with the moon's energy in your dreams. For example, if it's a full moon, say, "I invite the full moon's light into my dreams to guide me with clarity and truth." This simple act can help you form a stronger connection with the Moon and its influence over your dream life.

Dreams are full of symbols, and these symbols often carry messages from our subconscious mind. The moon's energy can make these symbols even more potent, revealing hidden truths and insights that can guide you in your magical practice. While every person's dreams are unique, there are some common symbols that appear in dreams and have special meanings, especially when influenced by lunar energy.

Seeing **water** in your dreams, such as oceans, rivers, or rain, often represents emotions and the flow of your subconscious. Water is closely tied to the moon, which controls the tides, so when water appears in your dreams, it might be the moon's way of encouraging you to pay attention to your feelings. If the water in your dream is calm, it could mean you're feeling peaceful and in harmony. If it's stormy or turbulent, it might indicate that you're going through emotional challenges or changes that need your attention.

Dreaming of the **Moon** itself is a powerful symbol. If you see the Moon in your dream, take note of its phase. A **full Moon** might symbolize a time of culmination, abundance, or emotional intensity, while a **new Moon** could suggest new beginnings, hidden potential, or a need for reflection. The Moon in dreams often acts as a guide, showing you the path toward deeper self-understanding and the cycles you're experiencing in your life.

Animals are another common dream symbol, and the specific animal can have different meanings. For example, a **wolf** might represent intuition, independence, and the call to explore your inner wildness, while a **cat** could symbolize mystery, magic, and the need to trust your instincts. The moon's energy can amplify the presence of these animals in your dreams, urging you to listen to their messages. If an animal appears in your dream, consider what qualities it represents and how those qualities might relate to your current experiences or challenges.

Sometimes, you might dream of **flying**, which can indicate a desire for freedom, exploration, or a higher perspective. The moon's influence on dreams of flying suggests that you're seeking to rise above your everyday concerns and connect with a more intuitive or spiritual viewpoint. This is especially true during the full moon, which heightens your emotions and desires to see things clearly.

Paying attention to the symbols in your dreams and how they connect with the moon's energy can help you uncover valuable insights about yourself and your magical path. Keep a dream journal to write down your dreams as soon as you wake up, noting any symbols, emotions, or messages you receive. Over time, you'll start to notice patterns and gain a deeper understanding of what your dreams are trying to tell you.

One of the challenges of working with dreams is remembering them. Dreams can be fleeting, slipping away like mist as soon as you wake up. However, with a few simple practices, you can train your mind to remember your dreams more vividly and use them in your magical practice.

The first step to remembering your dreams is setting the intention before you go to sleep. As you're lying in bed, take a few deep breaths, close your eyes, and say, "I will remember my dreams when I wake." Repeat this intention a few times, focusing on your desire to recall your dreams. This helps signal to your subconscious mind that you're open to receiving and remembering the messages that come through your dreams.

Keep a dream journal and a pen next to your bed. As soon as you wake up, before you move or get out of bed, take a moment to recall any images, feelings, or fragments of dreams. Even if you only remember a single word, color, or feeling, write it down. The more you practice this, the easier it will become to remember larger parts of your dreams. Over time, your mind will get used to this routine and start retaining more details.

You can also try placing a piece of moonstone or amethyst under your pillow while you sleep. These crystals are known for enhancing intuition and dream recall, and they help strengthen your connection to the moon's energy. As you hold the crystal before going to sleep, set the intention that it will help you remember your dreams. When you wake up, hold the crystal again and reflect on any dreams you had during the night.

Another trick for remembering dreams is to drink a small glass of water before bed. As you drink, say, "With this water, I open the doorway to my dreams." Water is a conductor of energy and is deeply connected to the moon, so using it in this way can help you tap into the moon's influence on your dreams. When you wake up, drink another sip of water and take a moment to recall your dreams, letting the water bring those memories to the surface.

Lunar dreams are a window into your subconscious, revealing hidden thoughts, emotions, and guidance that can enhance your magical practice. By understanding the moon's influence on dreams, exploring dream symbols, and using simple techniques to remember your dreams, you can tap into this mystical world and use it as a source of insight and inspiration. Each night is an opportunity to connect with the moon's energy, explore your inner world, and gather the wisdom that your dreams have to offer. As you embrace the magic of lunar dreams, you'll find that they become a powerful tool in your journey as a young witch, guiding you and helping you harness your true power.

Dream Magic

Dreams are one of the most magical parts of our lives. They can reveal hidden thoughts, answer questions we've been wondering about, and give us a peek into other realms of possibility. For witches, dreams are a powerful tool to explore our subconscious and connect with the moon's energy. When we're asleep, our minds are open to receiving messages from the universe, and the Moon plays a big role in guiding us through this dream world. In this chapter, we'll explore how you can dive into dream magic by creating a dream journal, casting lunar dream spells, and even calling on Moon spirits for guidance in your dreams.

A dream journal is one of the most valuable tools you can have as a Witch working with dreams. It's a special place where you can write down your dreams, keep track of dream symbols, and notice patterns over time. A dream journal is like a window into your inner world, showing you what your subconscious is trying to tell you. The more you use it, the more you'll be able to understand your dreams and use them in your magical practice.

To create your dream journal, find a notebook that you like and feels special to you. You can decorate the cover with Moon symbols, stars, or anything that reminds you of dream magic. If you prefer, you can also use a blank journal with no lines, so you have the freedom to draw symbols, sketch parts of your dreams, or write in any style you like. This is your magical space, so make it personal and inspiring.

Before you go to sleep each night, place your dream journal next to your bed with a pen or pencil. As you settle down, take a few moments to hold your journal and set an intention for remembering your dreams. You might say, "With this journal, I capture my dreams. I remember the messages the Moon sends to me." Setting this intention helps signal to your mind that you're open to exploring your dreams and remembering them when you wake up.

In the morning, before you get out of bed, take a moment to think about any dreams you had during the night. Even if you only remember a small part of a dream, a color, or a feeling, write it down in your journal. The key is to capture whatever you can, even if it seems like only a tiny fragment. As you get into the habit of writing down your dreams, you'll start to remember more details over time.

Write down everything you can recall about your dream: the places you visited, the people or creatures you saw, how you felt, and any symbols that stood out to you. Did you see a moonlit forest, fly through the stars, or meet a mysterious figure? All of these details are important, as they may carry messages from your subconscious or even from Moon spirits guiding you. Drawing pictures or symbols can also help bring your dream to life in the journal and might reveal new insights when you look back on them later.

By keeping a dream journal, you're creating a record of your journey through the dream world. Over time, you'll start to notice patterns and symbols that repeat in your dreams, giving you clues about your emotions, desires, and the guidance the Moon is offering you. This journal becomes a map of your inner landscape, helping you explore your magic more deeply.

Dream spells are a fun and powerful way to work with lunar magic while you sleep. These spells use the moon's energy to influence your dreams, guide you to answers, or help you connect with different realms of magic. When casting a dream spell, remember that the moon's phase can influence the kind of energy you're working with. For example, the full Moon is a great time for spells that seek clarity, while the new Moon is perfect for spells that invite new insights or beginnings.

One simple dream spell you can try is a **dream pouch**. To make this, gather a small piece of fabric (like a scrap of soft cloth) and some dried herbs known for their dream-enhancing properties, such as lavender, mugwort, or chamomile. Place the herbs in the center of the fabric, along with a small crystal, such as amethyst or moonstone, which are known for their calming and intuitive energy. If you have a Moon charm or a tiny moon-shaped object, add that to the pouch too. Fold the fabric around the herbs and crystal, tying it with a piece of ribbon or string to create a small pouch.

Before you go to bed, hold the dream pouch in your hands and close your eyes. Imagine the moonlight filling the pouch with magic and energy. Say, "Moon of night, guide my dreams. Show me the paths unseen. With this pouch, I call on thee, to bring me visions that I need to see." Place the pouch under your pillow, and let the moon's energy work while you sleep. In the morning, write down any dreams you remember in your journal, and keep the pouch in a safe place to use whenever you want to enhance your dream magic.

Another dream spell you can try is a **Moon water dream spray**. To make this, first create Moon water by placing a jar of water under the moonlight during a full Moon to absorb its energy. When you're ready to use it, pour a small amount of Moon water into a spray bottle and add a few drops of lavender or chamomile essential oil. Before you go to sleep, lightly mist your pillow with the Moon water spray, saying, "Moonlit mist, clear and bright, bring me dreams of magic tonight." This spell invites the moon's energy into your dreams, enhancing their vividness and clarity.

You can also use **crystals** in your dream spells. Place a piece of moonstone, selenite, or amethyst under your pillow before bed. As you do, say, "Crystal bright, guide my sight. Bring me dreams of peace tonight." These crystals are known for their calming, intuitive properties and can help guide your dreams, making them more memorable and meaningful.

Dreams are a powerful way to receive messages and guidance from Moon spirits. Moon spirits are magical beings that are said to live in the moonlight and the realms of dreams. They can appear as guides, protectors, or teachers, offering insight and wisdom as you explore your dream world. Calling on Moon spirits for guidance is a wonderful practice that can help you deepen your connection with the Moon and its magic.

To call on Moon spirits, start by creating a calming atmosphere in your room before bed. Light a white or silver candle on your altar to represent the moon's light, and place a crystal, like moonstone or selenite, nearby. Sit quietly for a few moments, holding the crystal in your hand, and take deep breaths to center yourself. Imagine the moon's light filling the room, creating a circle of soft, glowing energy around you.

Once you feel calm and focused, close your eyes and say, "Moon spirits, bright and true, I call upon your light. Guide me through the dream-filled night, show me visions pure and bright." Imagine the moon's light growing stronger, opening a doorway to the dream world. As you fall asleep, keep the intention in your mind that you're inviting the Moon spirits into your dreams to guide and protect you.

When you wake up, write down anything you remember about your dreams in your journal. Did you see any figures, animals, or symbols that felt meaningful? Did you receive a message, feeling, or guidance? Sometimes, Moon spirits appear as animals, glowing figures, or even as a feeling of comfort and protection within the dream. Trust your intuition and let yourself be open to their messages, even if they don't make sense right away.

You can also use Moon water to connect with Moon spirits before dreaming. Sprinkle a few drops of Moon water on your pillow and say, "Moon water, clear and bright, bring Moon spirits to me tonight. Show me the paths of dream and light, guide me through this magic night." This simple spell creates a bridge between your world and the realm of the Moon spirits, inviting them to join you in your dreams.

By working with Moon spirits, you can receive guidance, explore new realms of magic, and uncover deeper truths within yourself. Each time you call on them, you're strengthening your bond with the Moon and its magical energy.

Dream magic is a wonderful way for new Witches to explore their powers and connect with the moon's energy. By creating a dream journal, you're building a record of your subconscious thoughts and the guidance you receive in your sleep. Casting lunar dream spells helps you direct your dreams toward the insights and answers you seek, while calling on Moon spirits brings wisdom and guidance into your dream world. As you practice dream magic, you'll find that your dreams become a powerful tool for self-discovery, inspiration, and magical growth. Trust in the moon's light to guide you through the realm of dreams, and let your dreams light up the path of your witchcraft journey.

Nighttime Rituals

As a new witch, one of the most magical times for you to practice your craft is at night. The world gets quieter, the Moon shines brightly in the sky, and you can feel a different kind of energy surrounding you. Nighttime is perfect for connecting with your inner self, working with the moon's power, and setting the stage for magical dreams. In this chapter, you'll learn about nighttime rituals that will help you prepare for bedtime magic, cast sleep spells for peaceful dreams, and use moonlight meditation to drift into restful sleep.

Before diving into the magic of sleep spells and moonlight meditation, it's important to create a bedtime routine that sets the mood for nighttime magic. Preparing for bedtime magic is like telling your mind and body that it's time to relax and open up to the moon's energy. The more consistent your routine is, the stronger your connection with the Moon and your magic will become.

To prepare for bedtime magic, start by tidying up your space. Your room should feel like a calming sanctuary, so take a few minutes to clear away clutter, make your bed cozy, and dim the lights. Light a candle on your altar or bedside table to symbolize the moon's glow, or use a nightlight with a soft, cool color like blue or purple to create a soothing atmosphere. If you have a moon-themed lamp or a crystal lamp, even better! These little touches can help make your space feel magical and ready for your nighttime rituals.

Next, gather a few items that make you feel relaxed and connected to the moon's energy. This could be a piece of moonstone or amethyst, a small jar of Moon water, or even a favorite stuffed animal that brings you comfort. These items will serve as reminders of the moon's presence as you prepare for sleep. You can place them on your bedside table or under your pillow to keep them close as you drift off.

Once your space is ready, it's time to set your intention for the night. Take a moment to sit on your bed or in front of your altar, close your eyes, and take a few deep breaths. Imagine the moon's light filling your room, washing over you in a wave of calm, peaceful energy. Say to yourself, "I welcome the moon's magic into my dreams tonight. I am calm, safe, and open to the moon's guidance." This simple act sets the tone for the night, inviting peaceful, magical dreams to come your way.

After you've set up your space and intention, it's time to cast a sleep spell for peaceful dreams. Sleep spells are gentle, calming rituals that use the moon's energy to bring relaxation and encourage sweet, restful sleep. There are many different types of sleep spells, so you can choose one that feels right for you or mix and match elements from different spells to create your own.

One of the simplest and most effective sleep spells involves creating a **sleep sachet** filled with herbs and crystals known for their calming properties. To make a sleep sachet, gather a small piece of fabric or a drawstring pouch, dried lavender, chamomile, and a moonstone or amethyst crystal. Place the herbs and crystal in the center of the fabric, then tie the fabric together with a piece of string or ribbon to create a small pouch. Hold the sachet in your hands and close your eyes. Visualize the moonlight flowing into the pouch, filling it with peaceful energy. Say, "Moonlight bright, bring me dreams of peace tonight. Calm my mind, and let me rest, in sleep's embrace, I am blessed." Place the sachet under your pillow or beside your bed, and let the moon's magic work while you sleep.

If you have Moon water, you can also use it in a **sleep spell** to enhance the calming energy around you. Before bed, pour a small amount of Moon water into a bowl and place it on your bedside table or altar. Dip your fingers into the water and lightly sprinkle it around your bed, saying, "Moon water pure, bring me rest. Peaceful dreams at your request." This simple ritual creates a circle of Moon energy around your bed, inviting peaceful sleep and pleasant dreams. You can also rub a little Moon water on your wrists or forehead as you set your intention for a restful night.

Another lovely sleep spell involves using **essential oils** to create a relaxing atmosphere. Add a few drops of lavender or chamomile oil to a diffuser or a tissue placed near your pillow. As the scent fills the room, close your eyes and imagine the moon's light surrounding you in a soft, comforting embrace. Say, "Moon of night, scent so sweet, bring me dreams of calm and peace." This gentle spell uses the moon's magic and nature's scents to soothe your mind and body, helping you drift off to sleep.

Meditation is a powerful practice that helps calm your mind, relax your body, and prepare you for a restful sleep. A moonlight meditation is a special kind of meditation that uses the moon's energy to guide you into a state of deep relaxation. By focusing on the moon's light, you can clear away worries, quiet your thoughts, and invite peaceful dreams into your sleep.

To start your moonlight meditation, sit comfortably on your bed or a soft blanket on the floor. If you have a candle, light it to symbolize the moon's glow, or dim the lights in your room to create a calming atmosphere. Hold a piece of moonstone, amethyst, or selenite in your hands if you have one, as these crystals are known for their soothing and intuitive properties.

Close your eyes and take several deep breaths, inhaling slowly through your nose and exhaling through your mouth. As you breathe, imagine a beam of soft, silver moonlight shining down on you from above. Visualize this moonlight surrounding you, filling your room with a gentle glow. Feel the moon's energy washing over you like a cool, calming wave, easing away any tension or worries you've been carrying throughout the day.

As you continue to breathe, focus on the light of the moon. Imagine it pouring into your body, starting from the top of your head and slowly moving down to your toes. With each breath, feel the moonlight filling you up, bringing a sense of calm and peace. Let your body become heavy and relaxed, as if you're floating in a sea of moonlight.

If thoughts pop into your mind during the meditation, that's okay. Acknowledge them, then gently let them drift away like clouds passing through the sky. Bring your focus back to the moonlight and the feeling of peace it brings. You might silently say, "Moonlight bright, calm my mind. Bring me rest, dreams gentle and kind." This mantra helps you stay connected to the moon's soothing energy as you meditate.

When you're ready to end the meditation, take a few more deep breaths, then slowly open your eyes. If you've been holding a crystal, place it on your bedside table or under your pillow to keep its energy close while you sleep. Blow out your candle if you lit one, and thank the Moon for its calming presence. Feel free to stretch out on your bed, letting the relaxation from the meditation carry you gently into sleep.

Practicing moonlight meditation regularly can help you create a bedtime ritual that not only brings peaceful sleep but also strengthens your connection to the moon's energy. Over time, you'll find that your dreams become more vivid and meaningful, guided by the moon's light and magic.

Nighttime rituals are a wonderful way to embrace your magical practice as a new witch. By preparing your space for bedtime magic, casting sleep spells for peaceful dreams, and using moonlight meditation to relax, you're creating a nighttime routine that aligns with the moon's power and brings calm into your life. Each night is a chance to connect with the moon, invite its guidance into your dreams, and rest in its gentle embrace. With these rituals, you're not just falling asleep—you're entering a realm of magic where the Moon watches over you, guiding your dreams and filling your heart with peace.

PUTTING IT ALL TOGETHER

YOUR LUNAR MAGIC JOURNEY

You've learned so much about lunar magic and how to harness the moon's energy in your witchcraft. From creating a lunar altar to exploring dreams and practicing nighttime rituals, you now have a toolkit of magical practices to help you connect with the moon. But where do you go from here? The final step is putting it all together into a routine that suits you and helps you grow as a witch. Remember, your journey with Moon magic is unique. It's all about finding what feels right for you, trying different things, and building a practice that makes you feel connected and powerful. In this chapter, we'll explore how to create a Moon magic routine, combine lunar and star magic, and set goals for your witchcraft journey.

The moon's cycles give us a natural rhythm to follow in our magical practice. By building your Moon magic routine around these cycles, you can align yourself with the moon's energy, making your spells and rituals even more effective. But how do you start creating a routine that works for you?

First, think about what part of the moon's cycle resonates with you the most. Do you feel energized during the full moon, inspired by the new moon, or maybe calm during the waning phases? Identifying which phases you connect with will help you decide when to focus on different types of magic. For example, you might choose to set new intentions and goals during the new moon, work on attraction spells as the Moon waxes, celebrate your accomplishments during the full moon, and practice cleansing and releasing during the waning moon. Knowing which phase to work with allows you to plan your spells, rituals, and meditations in harmony with the moon's energy.

Next, choose one or two lunar practices to include in your routine. It's easy to feel overwhelmed when there are so many magical practices to try, so start simple. Maybe you want to do a new Moon ritual each month to set intentions, or perhaps you'd like to perform a full Moon meditation to connect with your inner wisdom. Pick practices that feel meaningful and enjoyable for you. As you get more comfortable with these routines, you can add more elements, like moon-phase altar rituals, dream journaling, or creating Moon water.

A great way to keep your Moon magic routine organized is by using a **Moon calendar.** A Moon calendar shows you the dates of the moon's phases and special events, like eclipses. By keeping track of the moon's cycle, you can plan your magical work in advance. For example, you can mark the full Moon as a day for a meditation or spell, and note when the new Moon arrives so you can prepare for intention-setting. You might even create your own Moon calendar in your journal, adding symbols, drawings, or notes about how you feel during each phase.

You might also want to create a **Moon magic journal** where you can write down your thoughts, feelings, and experiences throughout the moon's cycle. This journal can include your dream journal entries, notes from Moon meditations, spells you've tried, and reflections on your practice. Writing things down helps you see how your magic is evolving and shows you the patterns in how the Moon affects your energy and emotions.

Once you've established your basic routine, you can start experimenting with **star magic** to enhance your lunar practices. The Moon and stars have a special relationship in the night sky, and by combining their energies, you can create a more powerful magical practice. Star magic can guide you, offer inspiration, and help you tap into the vastness of the universe.

Start by learning about the **constellations** and finding your star sign in the sky. Your star sign, or zodiac sign, is connected to the position of the stars when you were born. Finding it in the sky can help you feel a deeper connection to the universe. Use a star map or a stargazing app to locate your star sign and other constellations. Once you've found your favorite stars, you can bring their energy into your Moon magic.

During your moon-phase rituals, include elements that represent the stars. For example, add star-shaped crystals or glitter to your altar, or draw constellations in your journal. When you perform a full Moon ritual, imagine the stars shining down on you, adding their light to the moon's energy. You can also call on the stars during Moon meditations by visualizing a sky filled with twinkling lights, each one offering guidance and magic.

For a simple star magic spell, gather a small jar, clear quartz, and a bit of silver glitter. Hold the jar under the night sky and whisper, "Stars above, shine your light. Bless this jar with magic bright." Place the quartz inside and sprinkle the glitter around it, imagining that you're capturing the stars' energy. Keep this jar on your altar and use it in spells to amplify your intentions or bring cosmic energy into your practice.

As you combine lunar and star magic, pay attention to how the moon's phases interact with the stars. Some Witches find that they feel different energies depending on which constellation the Moon is passing through. For example, when the Moon is in Leo, you might feel bold and creative, while a Moon in Pisces could bring about deep emotions and introspection. By tracking these changes in your journal, you'll gain a deeper understanding of how the Moon and stars work together in your magic.

Setting goals for your witchcraft is an important part of your journey. Just like setting intentions with the moon, having goals helps you stay focused, motivated, and excited about learning new things. These goals can be as big or small as you like. Maybe you want to learn how to read tarot cards, create your own Moon water rituals, or understand the moon's influence on plants and gardening. Whatever your goals are, they should reflect your interests and curiosity as a young witch.

Start by choosing a **main goal** for each Moon cycle. For example, during the waxing moon, you might set a goal to create a lunar talisman or learn about the properties of Moon crystals. During the full moon, focus on practicing a new spell or meditation technique. When the Moon wanes, set a goal to cleanse your altar, release old energy, or do some shadow work to explore your inner self.

It's also helpful to set **long-term goals** that span several Moon cycles. These might include developing a dream journal filled with insights, creating a detailed grimoire (your personal witchcraft guidebook), or building a strong relationship with Moon spirits and deities. Break these larger goals into smaller steps that you can work on each month. For example, if you want to create a grimoire, start by dedicating one Moon cycle to collecting information on Moon phases, another to writing down your spells, and another to designing the book's cover and pages.

Remember to **celebrate your progress**! Being a Witch is all about the journey, not just the destination. Each time you complete a goal, whether it's learning a new spell or simply sticking to your moon-phase rituals, take a moment to honor your achievement. Light a candle, do a short meditation, or give yourself a small treat. Acknowledging your progress helps you feel more confident in your practice and motivates you to keep exploring and growing.

Putting everything together into a practice that works for you is a magical experience. Your Moon magic journey is about finding what resonates with you, combining different elements, and learning how to flow with the moon's cycles. By creating a Moon magic routine, blending in star magic, and setting goals for your witchcraft, you're building a practice that is uniquely yours. Over time, you'll deepen your connection to the moon, the stars, and your inner magic, becoming more confident and empowered as a witch.

Remember, your journey with lunar magic is always evolving. Some Moon cycles, you might feel deeply connected to the moon's energy, while other times, you might need to take a step back and rest. Both are perfectly normal. Your practice doesn't have to be perfect; it just needs to be true to you. The Moon is a constant companion in the sky, shining down on you, offering its magic and guidance. So embrace your lunar path, follow your intuition, and let the moonlight guide you as you navigate the magical world of witchcraft.

STAYING CONNECTED TO THE MOON

As you continue your journey as a young witch, staying connected to the Moon will help you deepen your magical practice and develop a stronger bond with its ever-changing energy. The Moon is your constant companion in the night sky, a guiding light that influences your moods, dreams, and spells. Building a relationship with the Moon means learning to listen to its cycles, celebrate its phases, and honor its presence in your life. In this chapter, you'll discover how to keep a lunar journal, celebrate the moon's monthly phases, and create special seasonal lunar celebrations to enhance your magical connection.

Keeping a lunar journal is one of the most effective ways to stay in tune with the moon's energy. This journal is more than just a notebook; it's a sacred space where you can track the moon's phases, record your thoughts and feelings, document your dreams, and reflect on your magical experiences. Over time, your lunar journal will become a map of your inner world, showing how the moon's cycles affect you and your practice.

To start your lunar journal, choose a notebook that feels special. It could be a plain notebook that you decorate with Moon symbols, stars, and other magical elements, or a beautiful journal with blank or lined pages. What's most important is that it's something you'll enjoy writing in. If you like, dedicate the first page to a Moon blessing or a personal intention for your lunar journey. You might write something like, "With this journal, I honor the moon. I open my heart to its wisdom and light."

Use your journal to record the moon's phases and how they affect you. Each time the Moon enters a new phase—new moon, waxing crescent, first quarter, full moon, waning gibbous, third quarter, and waning crescent—make a note of it in your journal. Write down your feelings, thoughts, and any changes you notice in your mood or energy levels. You might feel more energized and creative during the waxing Moon or more introspective and emotional as the Moon wanes. By tracking these patterns, you'll start to understand how the moon's cycle aligns with your personal rhythms.

You can also use your lunar journal to explore your dreams, especially those that occur around the full Moon or new moon. Dreams can be powerful sources of guidance and insight, and writing them down helps you remember them and uncover their meanings. Each morning, take a few minutes to jot down any dreams you remember, along with any symbols, colors, or emotions that stood out to you. Over time, you'll notice patterns in your dreams that connect with the moon's phases, offering clues about your subconscious mind and your magical path.

Your lunar journal is also a place to document your rituals, spells, and meditations. Whenever you perform a Moon ritual—like creating Moon water, casting a full Moon spell, or doing a Moon meditation—write about the experience in your journal. Describe what you did, how you felt, and any messages or signs you received. This record will help you reflect on your practice, learn from your experiences, and see how your connection to the Moon grows over time.

Celebrating the moon's phases each month is a beautiful way to stay connected to its energy and honor its cycle. Each phase of the Moon has its own unique magic, offering different opportunities for reflection, intention-setting, and spellwork. By creating small rituals and celebrations for each phase, you can align yourself with the moon's energy and bring its magic into your daily life.

The **new Moon** marks the beginning of the lunar cycle and is a time for new beginnings, fresh starts, and setting intentions. To celebrate the new moon, create a small ritual that focuses on what you want to bring into your life during the coming month. Light a candle on your altar and sit quietly, holding a piece of moonstone or another crystal that symbolizes new beginnings. Close your eyes and take a few deep breaths, visualizing the darkness of the new Moon as a blank canvas. Think about what you want to create, grow, or change in your life. Write these intentions down in your lunar journal, or say them out loud. You might say, "Under the new moon's shadow, I plant the seeds of my intentions. May they grow strong and true."

During the **waxing Moon,** as the Moon grows from a sliver to full brightness, focus on building energy and working towards your goals. This is a great time to do spells that attract positivity, abundance, and growth. Celebrate this phase by adding elements to your altar that represent growth, such as fresh flowers, green candles, or a small bowl of seeds. Light a candle each evening and spend a few minutes visualizing your intentions growing stronger, just like the Moon in the sky. You might say, "As the Moon waxes, so do my dreams. I welcome growth and light into my life."

The **full Moon** is the peak of the lunar cycle, radiating energy, power, and clarity. This is a time of celebration, manifestation, and reflection. To honor the full moon, create a ritual that celebrates what you've accomplished and invites the moon's light to fill you with inspiration. Go outside and spend a few moments under the moonlight, feeling its energy wash over you. You might hold a piece of selenite or clear quartz and say, "Full Moon bright, fill me with your light. I honor my journey and embrace your power." If you have Moon water, place it under the full Moon to recharge it with its vibrant energy.

As the Moon begins to **wane**, shrinking in size each night, the energy shifts towards release, cleansing, and letting go. The waning Moon is the perfect time to focus on clearing out old energy, habits, or thoughts that no longer serve you. Create a simple ritual for the waning Moon by lighting a candle and placing a bowl of salt or water on your altar. Take a piece of paper and write down anything you wish to release—whether it's negative feelings, worries, or old patterns. Fold the paper and place it in the bowl, saying, "As the Moon wanes, I release what I no longer need. I cleanse my spirit and welcome the peace that follows." Leave the paper in the bowl overnight, then bury it in the earth or pour the water out in the morning to complete the ritual.

In addition to monthly Moon phase celebrations, you can also honor the Moon with special seasonal lunar celebrations throughout the year. These celebrations help you connect with the moon's cycle in relation to the changing seasons, enhancing your practice with the energy of nature. Each season brings a different kind of magic, and by tuning into these energies, you can deepen your connection to the Moon and the world around you.

In **spring**, the moon's energy is all about new growth, fresh beginnings, and renewal. To celebrate the spring moon, create a ritual that focuses on planting seeds—both physical and metaphorical. Gather some seeds, a small pot, and soil. As you plant the seeds, think about the intentions and goals you want to nurture in the coming months. Say, "Spring Moon bright, bless these seeds. Help them grow strong, like my dreams and needs." Place the pot on your altar or windowsill to remind you of the new beginnings you're inviting into your life.

Summer is a time of abundance, warmth, and energy. The moon's light is at its most vibrant, and this is a perfect time to celebrate your achievements and embrace the magic of the sun and Moon working together. Plan a moonlit walk or picnic under the summer moon. Bring along a piece of sunstone or citrine to honor the sun's energy and a moonstone to represent the moon. Spend time outside, soaking in the moon's light and expressing gratitude for the abundance in your life. You might say, "Summer moon, glowing bright, I honor your warmth and light. Thank you for the gifts you bring, as I dance and laugh in this summer ring."

In **autumn,** the moon's energy turns towards reflection, harvest, and preparation for rest. To celebrate the autumn moon, create a ritual that focuses on gratitude and letting go. Sit quietly at your altar, surrounded by autumn elements like leaves, acorns, or a small pumpkin. Light a candle and think about all that you've accomplished and experienced in the past months. Write down what you're grateful for in your lunar journal, then write down what you're ready to release as the year winds down. Say,

"Autumn moon, gentle and wise, I honor what I've gained, and what I release with open eyes."

During **winter**, the moon's light offers comfort, rest, and introspection. This is a time to celebrate the quiet magic of the Moon and the promise of new beginnings ahead. To honor the winter moon, create a cozy ritual at your altar. Light a white or silver candle and place a bowl of Moon water beside it. Hold a piece of amethyst or clear quartz in your hands and take deep breaths, feeling the calmness of the winter moon. Say, "Winter moon, quiet and deep, bring me peace as I rest and sleep. Guide me through the darkest night, until the new year brings fresh light."

Staying connected to the Moon is a journey filled with magic, discovery, and personal growth. By keeping a lunar journal, celebrating the moon's monthly phases, and honoring its presence through seasonal rituals, you create a practice that aligns you with the moon's rhythm. The Moon will always be there to guide you, lighting up your path with its changing phases. As you continue to explore lunar magic, let your connection with the Moon deepen, bringing more light, peace, and power into your life as a young witch.

Your Lunar Magic Path

You've been exploring the magic of the moon, learning how to harness its energy, and connecting with its phases in your life. Now, it's time to take everything you've learned and truly embrace your path as a Moon witch. This is an exciting part of your journey because it's where you start to shape your own unique practice. Being a Moon Witch isn't just about following rituals; it's about discovering who you are and how you connect with the moon's magic. In this chapter, we'll talk about how to embrace your Moon Witch self, share your Moon magic with others, and explore the next steps in advanced lunar magic.

Embracing your Moon Witch self means recognizing the magic inside you and letting it shine. It's about finding the confidence to trust your intuition, listen to your feelings, and connect with the Moon in a way that feels personal and powerful. This isn't always something that happens overnight; it's a journey of self-discovery that unfolds as you continue to practice and learn. You might already feel a special connection with the Moon whenever you look up at the night sky, or perhaps you feel most magical during certain Moon phases. These moments are your Moon magic showing up in your life, guiding you to explore more of who you are.

As a Moon witch, it's important to honor your unique style of magic. You might find that you prefer working with certain Moon phases over others, or that your rituals involve specific crystals, herbs, or symbols that resonate with you. Trust these preferences—they are clues to the kind of magic that works best for you. For example, if you love the energy of the full moon, you might focus your magic on celebration, abundance, and clarity during that time. If you feel most connected to the new moon, your practice might center around setting intentions, new beginnings, and self-reflection. The Moon is always changing, and so will your practice, depending on how you feel and what you need.

It's also helpful to create a small ritual to celebrate your identity as a Moon witch. This doesn't have to be anything elaborate; it can be as simple as lighting a candle on your altar and taking a few moments to acknowledge your journey. You might say, "I am a Moon witch. I embrace the moon's light and darkness. I honor its cycles and the magic within me." Speaking these words aloud reminds you of your connection to the Moon and your commitment to exploring your magical path. Keep this ritual as a part of your practice, returning to it whenever you need to boost your confidence or reconnect with your purpose.

Sharing your Moon magic with others is another exciting part of your journey. Magic is often more powerful when it's shared, and there's something special about connecting with other Witches and friends who are interested in the Moon and its energy. You can share your knowledge, learn from others, and even cast spells together to amplify the moon's power. There are many ways to share your Moon magic, and it's up to you to decide what feels right.

One simple way to share your Moon magic is by teaching a friend about the moon's phases and how they affect our energy. You could invite them to join you for a full Moon ritual or help them create their own lunar altar. Explain what you've learned about the different Moon phases and how they can set intentions during the new Moon or release negativity during the waning moon. Sharing this knowledge not only helps your friends understand the magic of the moon, but it also deepens your own practice. Teaching is a powerful way to explore your beliefs and strengthen your connection to the magic you're practicing.

If you feel comfortable, you could also invite friends over for a Moon gathering. This can be a small, cozy get-together during a special Moon phase, like the full Moon or a lunar eclipse. Set up your altar, light some candles, and provide a few crystals for everyone to hold. You might choose to do a group meditation, share your Moon water, or take turns expressing your intentions for the month. It's a wonderful way to bond with others and share in the moon's magic. Remember, there's no right or wrong way to host a Moon gathering; it's all about creating a space where everyone feels safe, inspired, and connected.

For those who might not know much about Moon magic, you can share your practice more subtly. Perhaps you could make moon-phase bookmarks as gifts or offer to make a Moon charm for a friend. You could also share some of your Moon water by giving them a small bottle with a note about how they can use it for peace and relaxation. Little gestures like these can introduce the magic of the Moon to others and show how you're incorporating lunar energy into your everyday life.

As you grow more confident in your practice, you might feel ready to explore advanced lunar magic. This doesn't mean you have to start doing complicated spells or rituals; it's about taking your practice to the next level by exploring deeper aspects of Moon magic. Advanced lunar magic can involve working with lunar deities, understanding astrology's connection to the moon, or learning to use the moon's energy for healing and manifestation.

One way to dive into advanced Moon magic is by exploring **lunar astrology**. The Moon moves through each zodiac sign about every two and a half days, and its position can influence the type of energy that's present. For example, when the Moon is in Aries, the energy might be bold, fiery, and perfect for taking action. When it's in Pisces, you might feel more dreamy, intuitive, and emotional. By tracking the moon's journey through the zodiac, you can time your spells and rituals to align with this energy. You might find that you prefer to perform specific types of magic, like creativity spells during a Moon in Leo or cleansing rituals during a Moon in Virgo.

Another way to explore advanced lunar magic is by working with **lunar deities** or **Moon spirits**. Many cultures have Moon deities, such as Selene, Artemis, or Hecate, who are associated with different aspects of the Moon and its power. If you feel drawn to a particular Moon goddess or spirit, you can incorporate offerings and prayers to them in your rituals. Light a candle in their honor, place symbols related to them on your altar, or meditate to connect with their energy. Building a relationship with a lunar deity can add a deeper layer to your practice, providing guidance, protection, and wisdom as you navigate your magical path.

You might also want to experiment with **lunar healing magic**, using the moon's energy to cleanse, heal, and restore balance. During the full moon, you can charge crystals and make Moon water specifically for healing purposes. Use these items in your self-care routines—drink Moon water for emotional clarity, place a charged crystal on your forehead for a soothing meditation, or add Moon water to your bath to cleanse away stress. The moon's light is gentle yet powerful, making it an excellent source of healing magic that you can incorporate into your practice in many ways.

Finally, as you explore advanced lunar magic, continue setting goals for your practice. Challenge yourself to learn new spells, deepen your meditation practice, or explore a new area of Moon magic each month. Set intentions for what you want to accomplish, and keep track of your progress in your lunar journal. The more you explore and experiment, the more you'll discover about yourself and your magical abilities.

Your journey as a Moon Witch is an ever-evolving path. By embracing your Moon Witch self, sharing your magic with others, and exploring new aspects of lunar magic, you're continuing to grow, learn, and connect with the moon's energy. Always remember that there's no right or wrong way to practice Moon magic—it's all about what feels true to you. The Moon is your guide and companion, lighting up your path and inspiring you to explore the depths of your own magic. Trust in its light, follow your intuition, and let your lunar journey unfold in its own beautiful, magical way.

Embracing
Your Moonlit
Magic

Congratulations, young witch! You've journeyed through the moon's phases, explored the stars, and learned how to harness the energies of the cosmos. As you finish this guide, remember that your magical path is only just beginning. Every spell, ritual, and moonlit moment you've explored here is a stepping stone on your journey to understanding your inner power and the magical world around you. Now, it's time to reflect on all that you've learned and look forward to the adventures still to come.

The Magic Within You

By now, you've seen how the Moon and stars can become your companions and guides in your witchcraft practice. You've learned how to align with the moon's cycles, create Moon water, and connect with lunar crystals. You've crafted star charms, built your lunar altar, and celebrated the magic of eclipses. Most importantly, you've tapped into the ancient rhythms of the universe and embraced the fact that you, too, are a part of this magical dance.

The Moon and stars have been there since the beginning of time, shining down on countless Witches before you. Just as they guided them, they are now here for you. This guide has given you the tools to begin your magical journey, but the real magic comes from within you. You hold the power to create change, manifest your dreams, and bring light into the world. Your intuition, your heart, and your inner wisdom are the most magical tools you possess. Always remember that the Moon may shine brightly in the night sky, but your light is just as strong and brilliant.

Your Lunar Practice Moving Forward

As you continue to explore your witchcraft, you may find yourself drawn to certain aspects of Moon and star magic. Perhaps you're fascinated by the phases of the Moon and how they influence your mood and energy. Maybe you feel a special connection with the stars, wishing upon them and finding comfort in their glow. Or, it could be the magic of lunar crystals, the joy of making Moon water, or the serenity of your moonlit altar that calls to you.

Whichever path you take, remember that your practice is uniquely yours. There's no right or wrong way to be a Moon witch. Some months, you might find yourself performing detailed full Moon rituals, while other times, simply gazing up at the stars with a quiet intention might be all you need.

Your magic is personal, and it changes as you do. Trust in your instincts, and let your practice flow naturally.

As you grow and learn, your relationship with the Moon and stars will deepen. Keep your Moon journal handy, jotting down your thoughts, spells, and experiences. Use it to reflect on what works for you and what feels most magical. Over time, you'll see patterns emerge—times when you feel most powerful, spells that resonate deeply, and rituals that bring you the greatest peace. These reflections will help guide you as you continue to develop your practice.

Exploring New Magical Horizons

This guide has provided a foundation for your journey with lunar and celestial magic, but remember, there's always more to explore! The universe is vast, and magic is endless. Now that you've begun to understand the rhythms of the Moon and stars, consider expanding your practice into new realms of witchcraft.

You might find yourself curious about other forms of elemental magic, working with earth, fire, water, and air. Or perhaps you want to delve deeper into astrology, learning about your sun sign, Moon sign, and how the stars influence different aspects of your life. Crystal magic, herbal spells, divination, and dream magic are just a few more areas waiting for you to explore.

The Moon and stars are just one part of the magical tapestry. They serve as a gateway to deeper knowledge and understanding. Don't be afraid to follow where your curiosity leads. Remember, every witch's journey is unique, and your magic will continue to grow as you do.

Celebrating Your Magical Self

The magic of the Moon and stars isn't just about rituals and spells. It's also about learning to celebrate yourself and the world around you. The Moon teaches us to embrace all of our phases—the new, the full, the waxing, and the waning. It reminds us that it's okay to change, to grow, and to rest when needed. The stars encourage us to dream big, to reach for the impossible, and to believe in the magic within ourselves.

So, as you walk this path, remember to honor and celebrate who you are. You are a Moon witch, a star seeker, and a magical being with the power to create, transform, and illuminate. Your light is as constant as the stars, as shifting as the moon, and as beautiful as the night sky. Embrace it. Celebrate it. Use it to shine light and love into the world.

Your Moonlit Future

Now that you've journeyed through this guide, you're equipped with the knowledge and tools to weave magic into your everyday life. Whether it's a small daily ritual, a monthly full Moon celebration, or simply taking a moment to gaze up at the stars, you have the power to create magic whenever you need it.

Your future as a Witch is bright and full of wonder. As you continue to grow and learn, the Moon and stars will be your constant companions, guiding and supporting you. Remember to keep an open heart, listen to your intuition, and let the universe show you the way.

If you ever feel uncertain or lost, just look up at the moon. Let her remind you of your journey, your magic, and the power you hold within. The Moon is always there to light your path, just as the stars are there to guide your dreams. And now, you are a part of that cosmic magic—a young Witch with the universe at your fingertips.

A Final Note: Stay Curious, Stay Magical

As you close this book, know that this is not an ending but rather a new beginning. Your journey into the world of lunar and star magic is ongoing, filled with discoveries, growth, and endless enchantment. The Moon and stars are just the start of your magical path, and the more you explore, the more magic you'll find.

Stay curious. Keep learning, dreaming, and experimenting. Magic is as much about the journey as it is about the destination. It's about finding joy in the small things, like a quiet night under the stars or the glow of the full moon. It's about embracing your inner witch, trusting in your power, and knowing that you are enough—just as you are.

So, go forth, Moon witch. Gaze up at the night sky, breathe in the magic of the universe, and let your light shine. The world needs your magic. The Moon and stars are waiting. And now, you are ready to embrace it all.

Blessed be, and may the moonlight guide you always.

Meet Wilhelmina

Wilhelmina Woods hails from a rich lineage of Witches, Healers, Shamans, and Wise Women on both her mother's and father's sides, with the occasional nun adding a surprising twist to her family tree. Raised in an openly spiritual home alongside her four younger sisters, she was always encouraged to embrace her true self. For Wilhelmina, this meant wholeheartedly embracing her Witch heritage. Her sisters—River, Sage, Raven and Willow—are also authors, each following their own unique path. Wilhelmina, with pride and passion, carries on the family's magical legacy.